A KILLING IN KANSAS

A MOUNTAIN MAN STORY

GEORGE M. GOODWIN

For information contact: info@outlawspublishing.com
Cover Art by Michael Thomas
Cover design by Outlaws Publishing LLC
Published by Outlaws Publishing LLC
June 2024
10987654321

Leaving Leavenworth

Everett Evers sat on his horse and looked down at the valley floor far beneath him. Although the rider he watched was nearly a half-mile below him and some ten miles from where the switchback trail started up the mountain, he knew exactly who the rider was. He knew by the way he sat in the saddle, by the horse he rode, and by the fact that Everett had been expecting him to show up anytime now. If he still carried that old Sharps .50-caliber he'd used during his buffalo hunting days, he could end all of this right here and now. The fact that Everett didn't have the rifle, and that he had not and would never shoot a man from cover, rendered that thought useless.

As he turned that little tan-colored horse of his up the steep and winding trail, he told himself to just keep avoiding the man. "If and when he catches up, then he will have brought it on himself. Let's see how that fat old Morgan of his likes this high-up country," he told Mouse. That little horse of his had been born in country like this, and he took to it like a pig to mud. Chance Mason rode out in the open without fear. He would have done so even if he'd known he was being watched. He knew the man he trailed had carried no heavy rifle since his buffalo hunting days had ended. Besides, he didn't believe Everett would use it on him even if he'd still had it. He had known Everett since they were children.

They were about ten years old when Everett and his ma had moved to the town of Leavenworth. Chance had been born there, and his father was the sheriff of Leavenworth. As boys, the two of them, among others, had fished the same streams, and hunted the same woods together. Everett had always been better at tracking, shooting, and pretty much everything, but he never bragged. Things just seemed to come to him without really trying.

A few years later, the boys had fought over the same girls more than once but remained friends. It seemed like there were always too many boys and too few girls in Leavenworth. That was okay though, at least to the girls, because it made the boys work that much harder to impress them. There had been a time back then that

Chance had thought of Everett Evers as a brother. In the year 1870, two things happened that would change all that, maybe forever. The boys were seventeen at the time and finding their way to becoming men. With the war between the states having been over for some five years, things were finally beginning to find their way back to something close to normal. More and more people were heading west. Many of them had lost everything in the war, and many others were impressed by the tall tales of wandering men who had been there. There were stories of wide-open land for the taking, and game that practically killed and dressed itself.

Because of all these people going west, the government found itself needing to send more and more soldiers out there to protect them. This meant building new forts for all those soldiers, which was only fanning the flames of hatred from the Indians, giving them more reason to rise up against the flood of whites coming into their lands. All of these new soldiers would have to be fed something, and the leaders in Washington decided that buffalo meat would be the closest, easiest, and cheapest thing for the government to obtain. Also, back in the East, there was a big demand for the robes of the animals, and the tongues had become something of a delicacy in many of the restaurants there. The rest would be taken to the nearest fort, from where they were hunted and distributed to other forts in the area. The leaders in Washington saw hunting the buffalo as solving two problems at once; it not only fed the many soldiers sent there, but also deprived the Indian people of them. The Indians had relied on the buffalo for almost everything in their lives for hundreds of years.

As the boys had grown older, their paths seem to lead in different directions. Everett had experienced several run-ins with the sheriff. It was never anything serious, just too much drinking and fighting. Struggling to find his way to being a man was not easy, and not having a pa to help him made it even harder for Everett. He had spent a few nights in the local jail.

Early in the year 1870, Everett and two other boys took a job for a local man clearing some land to get it ready for building. When the job was finished, the man told them he was not going to pay them. When Everett asked him why, he had said simply, "Because I don't have to." The other two boys weren't happy about it, but they chalked it up as a lesson learned. In the future, they would be more careful about who they worked for.

Everett didn't see things that way. He had worked and worked hard for that money, and he meant to have it. The night after the job was finished, Everett was in the saloon, having what looked like would probably be his last beer for a while, when the man he had worked for walked in. He took a stool at the bar, away from Everett, and ordered a whiskey. Everett watched as the man pulled a roll of bills from his pocket to pay for the drink. Everett turned to the cowboy beside him and very loudly asked what the cowboy thought of somebody that would work other men for weeks, doing work that they themselves were either too lazy or too stupid to do, then, when the job was finished, refuse to pay them for their labor, not because there was a problem with the work, but just because he didn't want to.

"I believe that would be a real sorry excuse for a man," the cowboy replied.

"Well, sir," said Everett, "we have such a man in this

town. In fact, we have such a man in this saloon at this very time. A man who gets what he wants by bullying others."

Many of the men in the saloon knew who Everett and the other boys had been working for, and some of them had even heard that he had refused to pay the boys. Otis Cummins sat and listened, until he had heard all he intended to hear from this bigmouth kid. When he had heard enough, he came off his stool and headed down the bar. Everett was on his feet and waiting for him when he got there. Otis was six inches taller than Everett's five feet, ten inches and outweighed him by a good eighty pounds at least. As a big man, Cummins had used that size most of his life to push people around and get what he wanted. If you said he was liked by anybody in town, you'd be telling a lie. Most people simply tolerated him or were scared of him. Everett was not of a mind to tolerate or to be scared.

Cummins never said a word as he walked up to Everett, he just swung as he came close enough. He was close enough, but he was a long way from being fast enough. Everett sidestepped the blow and punched Otis in the face. He hit Otis twice before the big man could get set for him. Otis swung again, with first his huge right hand, and then his left. Everett ducked them both and went in on the big man's midsection. Everett had worked hard all his life to support his mother and himself, and in the last couple of years had fought with a good many men. He had taken several pretty bad beatings to start with, but with each fight he had learned something new.

He was the kind of person that if he ever learned something, it stayed with him. Although he was outsized by Cummins, he had speed, strength, and age on his side. Each blow to the big man's stomach brought an exhaust of air from his lungs. Before long, sensing that he might be in trouble for the first time in his life, Otis swung hard with his left hand, hoping to end it quickly. Everett wasn't able to get completely out of the way. The blow caught him on his left shoulder. Instead of fighting against the blow, Everett let it take him in a full sweeping circle, and when he again faced Otis, he was ready. His hard right fist caught Otis Cummins square on Cummins' left jaw. The crack of that jawbone breaking could be heard all over the saloon. The big man's eyes went wide, rolled back in his head, and he pitched forward on the floor, out cold. Bending over, Everett reached into the pocket, from which he had earlier seen Cummings take money to pay for the drink.

Everett pulled out a rather large wad of bills. Then, with every eye in the place on him, he counted out the amount that was owed to him. He crammed the rest of the money back in the same pocket he'd taken it from and walked out of the saloon.

Sheriff Mason was knocking at their door early the next morning and had arrested him for assault and robbery. For the next eight days, Everett sat in jail. He had tried many times to tell his side of what had happened, and why it happened to the sheriff. The sheriff's only reply had been, "Tell it to the judge when he gets here."

On the morning of the ninth day of Everett's being locked up, Sheriff Mason came in with Everett's breakfast and told him that his mother had died sometime during the night. He knew his ma had been sick for quite a while, and he had taken the job that got him where he was now to make life a little easier for both of them in her final weeks. Everett did everything but beg the sheriff to let him out of jail just long enough to attend to his mother's burial, promising that when she was buried, he would turn himself back in. Not only was he not let out, but the sheriff wouldn't even take him to the funeral, even when he'd told the sheriff he would go handcuffed if that was the way the sheriff wanted it.

Sheriff Mason said, "no," and started in on Everett about how if he hadn't been in so much trouble for most of his life, things would be different. He told the sheriff that it was okay, but that someday the sheriff would pay for his actions.

Three days after his mother was buried, the judge made it to town. The morning of his hearing, fourteen men showed up to testify that not only had Otis Cummins started the fight at the saloon with Everett that night, but that he had refused to pay Everett and two other boys for work they had done for him. The nonpayment was what had caused the fight. The men told the judge that Everett had not robbed Otis; he had merely taken the wages owed to him for the work performed.

The men stated that Everett had then returned the rest of the money to Cummins' pocket. The judge had heard some years before what kind of a man Otis Cummins was, and that, along with the many witnesses, made the judge decide that he wasn't about to get caught up in a long, drawn-out case. Instead, he dismissed all charges against Everett, then turned and ordered Otis to pay the other two men for their labor, or he would see to it that Otis was run out of town on a rail.

When it was over, the sheriff never once told Everett he was sorry for the treatment he had received when his mother had died. He looked at the judge with disgust, and shaking his head, he walked out.

It was only a few days after the trial that a man showed up in town looking for men who could shoot and wished to go west. Everett was the first one to sign up and was told he would be hunting buffalo to supply food for soldiers. He and three others from Leavenworth would end up going.

Everett had tried to talk Chance into going, but Chance refused, saying that he had other plans right there in town. The company had a contract with the government to supply meat to the forts already built and being built out west, they were told. Each of the shooters was to be issued a brand new Sharps .50-caliber rifle, which was the newest model. Each man would also have a wagon following them with a skinner and a butcher in it. They were expected to do nothing but find and kill animals.

They would be paid a dollar for each buffalo they killed. It was specified, though, that the company wanted only full grown buffalo; male or female made no difference. If the shooters wished to, or accidentally, shot a calf, they could keep it for themselves. Under no circumstances were they to trade the meat or hides with local Indians. They could eat it themselves, or just take the hide, but they were not allowed to give it to the Indians. Being the good shot that he was, Everett was soon making upward of a hundred dollars on a good day. He had no way of knowing then, but it would be three long years before he next rode into his hometown of Leavenworth, Kansas.

A lot of the shooters would take a break occasionally

and go into whatever town they were closest to at the time to drink and gamble. Knowing his own history, Everett did not go with the other shooters. In fact, after a while, when another shooter was going to town for a few days, Everett would ask their skinner and butcher to stay. If they were willing, Everett would keep two wagons running until the other shooter came back. He grew quiet, accustomed to being alone out on the plains. Not all men could adjust to being alone so much, but Everett found he liked it very well. While he was working with two wagons during his third year, one of the wagons had left for town, and the other was almost fully loaded. Everett topped a little rise and saw a small herd below him that was mostly older cows.

He figured to finish the second wagon with these, and then rest until the next day when the crew would start again. The fourth big cow he dropped didn't seem to die instantly like most of them, so Everett drew up beside her and got down to check her before the skinner got there. The skinner and butcher carried no guns, and he didn't want to take a chance that she wasn't fatally wounded. He rarely missed a kill shot, but maybe it had been a short load of the shell or something. He had been looking down at the old cow and had never even seen the bull charging at him until the last moment. That bull must have weighed nearly a ton. He tried to sidestep the great shaggy head of the charging animal, and came close to being successful, but as the saying goes, "Close only counts in horseshoes."

A curved black horn of that bull hooked him about two inches from the center of his stomach, and as he was spinning to get out of its way, the horn tore a gash from where it entered his body, almost around to his spine. Everett hit the ground and looked up to see the beast coming at him again. He grabbed his rifle, and knowing he would only get one chance, waited until the bull was no more than five or six feet away from him to fire. Its front legs buckled, and when the bull had stopped sliding, that massive head was mere inches from where he lay propped up on his left arm. The wound wasn't so deep as to have hit anything vital, however, the sheer size of it had him bleeding very badly.

Everett knew that if he didn't act fast, he would bleed to death right there on that Texas plain. He took off his coat and belt, and quickly rolled the coat and wrapped it around himself and over the wound. Then, he drew the belt around and over the top of the coat and pulled it as tight as he could to buckle it. At about that same time, the wagon drew up beside him and seeing the blood everywhere, the two men came off the seat on the run.

"Bull hooked me," Everett told the skinner as he reached Everett's side.

"Very bad?" the skinner asked.

"Nearly halfway around me," said Everett.

"We have to get you to town," said the butcher.

"Tighten this belt some more before you load me," said Everett.

He was unconscious from the loss of blood by the time they finally made it into town and would not wake up for three days following their arrival. The doctor had worked on him for nearly five hours, he was told later, and had put in over two hundred stitches to close the wound. They had reached town before Everett's own wagon had started back out, and the drivers talked to each other and explained what had happened. They told

Everett's team to go get the other cows and that bull, then come right back because Everett would be down for a while, or maybe forever.

Twelve days later, Everett Evers was back on the plains hunting buffalo. For three months longer, he hunted. Then, at the end of a good day when he had shot eighty buffalo, he sat by his fire and decided he'd had enough.

Early the next morning, he told the butcher and the skinner. He thanked his own skinner and butcher for their service to him, and also sent word of thanks to the men that had brought him to town the day he was injured. Then, he rode away from the plains of Texas in a northeasterly direction, back to Kansas.

The first place he went when he rode back into Leavenworth after over three years, was to the cemetery. He had hired, by wire, a stonecutter to carve a headstone for his mother's grave after his first month on the plains, and he wanted to make sure that had been done.

The second place he went was the office of the company that he had worked for these last years. Everett looked nothing like the boy who had left this town three years ago. He now wore all buckskin clothing, and even knee-high Indian moccasins, like the ones favored by the Apaches. He wore a pistol on his left hip, butt forward, and a large bone handled knife on the right.

He had traded ten calf hides to another shooter for that knife. His face and arms were now as dark as any Indian. Only his blond hair and sky blue eyes told that he was not an Indian, and both his hair and eyes seemed bleached even lighter by the sun of the plains and stood out against the copper color of his skin. His first night in town, he went for a beer, and at the saloon he sat with men who had known him most of his life, but now had no idea who sat beside them. The quick temper of his youth was all but gone. Almost gone, but not completely, as another shooter on the plains had found out one time.

The following morning, he headed for the sheriff's office. He was hoping to find where Chance might be living. Someone had said the previous night that Chance was now his father's deputy and had been for the past two years. Before Everett got to the office, he saw a girl he had courted some time before leaving Leavenworth.

As they passed, he spoke her name. His looks may have changed, but Angie Washburn would never forget that voice. Spinning on her heels, she asked, "Everett, is that really you?"

"It is," he said, "or what's left of me."

"Where in the world have you been?" she asked.

"Out on the plains of Texas, mostly," he told her. "How have you been? Can I buy you a cup of coffee, so we can talk a while?"

"I can't right now," she said. "I'm working over at the general store, and old man Jinx will give me the devil if I'm late."

"Well, how about supper this evening? Are you free?" he asked.

"I get through at five," she replied.

"I'll be waiting out front," he said.

She walked toward the store, and he continued to the sheriff's office. When he went in the door, Chance was behind the desk digging in a drawer for something. It appeared his father wasn't there yet, and Everett was glad. His dislike for the elder Mason was still very much in his mind.

Looking up from his hunt, Chance said, "Can I help you?"

"I guess not," said Everett. "I was looking for an old friend, but I guess he must have forgotten me."

"Everett!" Chance exclaimed, coming around the desk. "By God, it's good to see you!" he said, shaking hands so hard Everett thought his arm might come off. "We heard, last year, that you were dead," said Chance, "but I told them all there was no way. I told them you were too damn mean to die."

"Came close," said Everett.

"How's that? What happened?" Chance asked him.

Everett pulled up his buckskin shirt to reveal a scar from the center of his stomach nearly around to his backbone, just under the ribcage. "Dropped a big old cow and as I was looking her over to be sure she was dead, I let a bull get in too close. Sometimes their size makes you forget just how fast they are," Everett said.

"Man alive," said Chance. "Well, other than that how have you been?"

"Good," replied Everett. "Stayed away from towns mostly, and just hunted all day and slept out under the stars at night. What about you? You're a deputy now, I hear. Hell, it seems like you used to get in as much trouble as I did."

"Nobody got in as much trouble as you did," said Chance. How about supper tonight?"

"Matter of fact, I just made plans," said Everett.

"Anybody I know?" asked Chance.

"Sure," Everett said. "You remember Angie, don't you?"

"Angie Washburn?" asked Chance.

"Yeah, said Everett, "I bumped into her on the street a few minutes ago. Say, why don't we all go together? Just old friends catching up on old times."

"You two go ahead," said Chance, "I'm sure the two of you have a lot of catching up to do. Besides, I never know what time I'll finish here. Since hiring me on, Pa has starting to do less around here."

"Maybe tomorrow night then," said Everett.

"Sure," said Chance, "sounds great."

"All right, Buddy, I'll see you later," said Everett.

He met Angie in front of the store at five. *She sure looks fresh to have worked all day*, he thought. She took his arm as they headed toward the diner, and neither of them were aware of a certain pair of eyes that followed their every step.

At the diner, Everett told her to order whatever she wanted. "I heard you had made a lot of money out there," she said. "I'm just surprised you didn't spend it all on saloon girls and drinking."

"Actually," he told her, "Last night at the saloon was the first drink I've had since the day I rode away from here three years ago, and you are the first girl I've talked to in the same amount of time."

As they waited for their food, she asked what Texas was like and about his work. "It's big," he said, "and flat, or so it appears. Sometimes you can look out across the plains, and it's there for as far as the eye can see in every direction. Then, you go riding across it and find a valley. Some of them big enough to hide this town in. When you ride up out of the valley, the country looks flat again."

"Maybe I was waiting for you to come back," she said.

"That's not very likely," Everett said. "As I recall, you had dropped me from your dance card before I had even left Leavenworth."

"I had no choice," she said. "You were usually in jail when the dances were being held. To be honest, I have been seeing someone regular."

"Maybe that should have been my first question," he told her. "Anybody I might know?" he asked.

"Sure, you know him," she said. "The two of you were like brothers growing up."

"You mean Chance Mason!" he almost shouted. "I went to see him right after I saw you this morning. I invited him to have supper with us, but he said he had to work late."

"That must have been a little uncomfortable," she said.

"Yeah," Everett replied, "a little bit." *Well,* he thought, *it's all innocent enough, but he should have spoken up when I told him, or he should have come along like I asked him to.*

This would change his plans for later, though, as he had hoped to get really reacquainted with Angie Washburn. He would not do that to a friend. By the time their meal was over, the night had grown dark, and he ask if she still lived with her folks. "Same place," she said, "but both Ma and Pa passed away about two years ago."

"Sorry to hear that," he said. "They were good people."

"I'm there all by myself now," she told him. When they reached the door, he told her he had enjoyed the evening but should be going. "I did tell you about Ma and Pa, didn't I?"

"You did," said Everett, "and you also told me about you and Chance."

"Well, it's not like we're married yet," she said.

"It's close enough for me. I'll see you around, Angie," he said as he turned to go.

"Don't go to the trouble," she called after him.

Everett walked toward the saloon on the pitch black street. As he passed an alleyway, a voice said, "How about buying a drink for a man down on his luck, friend?" Everett spun around, and a large man lumbered from the dark alleyway. "What do you say about that drink?" he asked Everett.

"I've been down before myself," Everett said, and reaching in his pocket, he flipped a silver dollar to the man. He went in the saloon and sat down on a stool about halfway down the bar. The doors opened right after he sat down, and the man he'd given the dollar to came in.

"Get out of here, Otis," said the barkeep. "What have I told you about coming in here, sponging drinks, and bothering my customers?"

"I have money this time," the man told him, producing the dollar, and sitting down on a stool.

"Whiskey?" asked the barkeep.

"That's right," said the man, "and you can leave the bottle."

"You haven't got enough for a bottle," said the barkeep as the man tossed off his whiskey.

"Then just give me another whiskey," said the big man.

When he finished drinking and left, Everett called the barkeep over for another beer. "Did I hear you call that man 'Otis'?" he asked.

"That's right," the barkeep said, "Otis Cummins. He's been nothing but a drunk ever since I started here, but I've been told he used to be a powerful man around these parts. Owned a lot of property and had quite a bit of money. That is until some kid beat him down over some money he owed to the kid and refused to pay. It happened right here in this saloon. When Otis took this kid to court, he got beat down again by the judge. A year or so later, he lost his wife.

"It's rough on a man when his spouse dies," Everett responded.

"Oh, she didn't die." The barkeep continued, "She

left him for the man that used to tend bar here. I'll get your beer."

*

The next morning, Everett walked over to the sheriff's office, and Sheriff Charlie Mason was there. "Can I help you?" the sheriff asked as Everett walked in.

"I was looking for Chance," Everett said.

"He's out running some errands," replied the sheriff, "but he'll be back in a couple of hours."

"Thanks," said Everett.

"Can I tell him you came by?" asked the sheriff.

"Sure," Everett told him, "That would be great."

"Well, I'll need a name," the sheriff said.

"It's me, Sheriff Mason," he said, "Everett Evers."

"Evers," said the sheriff, "Boy, I would never have recognized you. Last I heard you was killed down on the Texas plains."

"Not dead," Everett told him, "Just got hooked by a big bull and messed up pretty bad."

"How long you been back in town?" asked the sheriff.

"A couple of days," Everett replied.

"I guess a better question is, how long are you planning to stay?" the sheriff responded.

"Just came to see some old friends. I won't be staying long, Sir."

"I don't want no trouble," the sheriff told Everett.

"You don't have to worry about that," Everett said.

"Didn't say I was worried about it," said the sheriff, "just that I didn't want any."

"Yes, sir," Everett said and went out the door.

*

He was sitting in the diner at noon having some lunch, when

Chance walked in. "Howdy," Chance said, "I heard you had a run-in with Pa this morning."

"I saw him," said Everett, "but if there was a run-in, it was on his part, not mine."

"Just the same," Chance said, "I guess you'd better not come by the office anymore."

"Not even if I need a sheriff, or a deputy?" Everett asked.

"So how was your date last night?" Chance asked, changing the subject.

"It wasn't a date. I told you, it was just two old friends having a meal together. Chance, why didn't you tell me you and her are an item?" replied Everett.

"Would it have mattered?" asked Chance.

"Frankly, no," Everett told him. "I was just having supper with an old friend. I invited you to come with us, and you refused."

"You going to see her again?" Chance asked.

"No," Everett said, "in fact, I guess I'll pack up and leave. I came back here looking to see some old friends, but all I've found so far are people keeping secrets from me and then treating me like I've done something wrong, without me even knowing what it is I've done."

"Well, it's a free country," said Chance. "If you want

to ride, then ride.”

"Go to hell," Everett told him.

"Now, you might want to watch that kind of talk. You know, you're talking to a deputy sheriff," Chance said. By now he was beginning to get mad.

"Deputy Sheriff?" Everett replied. "All I see is your pop's errand boy. Are you going to arrest me yourself?"

"I just might, at that," Chance said.

"There's never been, and will never be, a day you want to try that, Chance Mason, or your pa will be back to running his own errands."

"I think you really need to ride out," said Chance. Then he turned and walked out of the diner.

Everett wasn't really sore with Chance, because he knew that the whole problem was that his old man had started on him as soon as Chance had gotten back to the office. He was sure Chance had gotten an earful about Everett, just like he always had. Everett could just hear the sheriff saying, "Now, Chance, you can't be hanging out with the likes of him anymore. After all, you're a deputy sheriff now."

Chance left the diner, and went to the company to turn in his rifle and draw his last pay. They all seemed very surprised when he told them he was done, and he was told that everyone thought he had liked his job. "I did," he told them, "And I appreciate it, but ever since that bull got me, I been figuring to get out."

"Well, you've done good by us," the company man told him, "And if you change your mind later, just come on back."

"I'll do that," Everett said, "but I hope to be going farther west. Maybe I'll even go all the way to California."

The company man counted out thirty-two one hundred dollar bills, and he put it into Everett's pocket. "I'll see you," Everett said and walked out.

From there, he went to the saloon and had a beer for the road, then went to the hotel and up to his room. As soon as he walked in, he knew somebody had been in there. With a little checking, he found a hundred dollars he always kept poked back in his bag for hard times, gone, and his big bone handled knife was missing. For an instant, he thought about going to the sheriff to report the robbery. Then he remembered where he was.

After what had just happened an hour ago with Chance, he knew he'd get no help from them. With the money he had just collected, he had nearly five thousand dollars on him and another knife as well. He also had money banked from the years before but had no need of it now. *I just want to get out of here,* he thought.

He stopped at the front desk, paid his bill, then went to the stable and saddled his horse, Mouse. As he led him from the stable, a voice behind him said, "I know who you are now, boy." He turned around to find Otis Cummins standing there.

Cummins continued, "You may think so, Evers, but that dollar you gave me last night don't make us square. Not in my book and not by a long shot."

"I never thought that." Everett said. "As far as I'm concerned, I squared me and you three years ago, Cummins. To be honest, I didn't even know who you were last night. Now, if you'll excuse me, I'm just leaving. Frankly, right now I don't care if you take over or burn down the whole damn town." He climbed on that little horse of his and never looked back. He was through with Leavenworth, as much as it seemed to be through with him.

*

He rode the sun out of the sky and then found a likely place to stop for the night. "I'll have to admit, my cooking held no candles to that lady at the diner, Mouse, but the company is better than I've had the last few days." He slept better that night than he had in a while; in fact, since he was on the plains. He was up and in the saddle early the next morning.

As he was about to hit the main road, he heard horses coming at a fast pace. They rode up to him in a cloud of swirling dust, and as it settled, he saw that there were three riders holding pistols on him. Chance Mason was in the front, and he told Everett to unbuckle his gun belt and let it fall.

"What's this all about?" Everett asked him.

"You know what it's about," Chance said very loudly.

"Because I called you an errand boy?" Everett asked.

"You killed Pa last night," said Chance.

"You're out of your mind!" Everett exclaimed. "I left town not two hours after you invited me to, and I didn't stop until I camped for the night right back there in the trees."

"A bone handled knife sticking out of Pa's chest tells me a different story," Chance said. "There were several people in town who saw you wearing that knife, when you first showed your face there."

"That was stolen from my room before I left town," Everett stated. "That knife and a hundred dollars I always kept hidden."

"I think you're a liar," said Chance.

"I really don't give a damn what you think right now," Everett told him. "We have a lot of history behind us, Chance, but if you ever call me a liar again, badge or no badge, I'll kill you."

"Everett, I'm only going to tell you one more time to shuck that gun belt," Chance said.

Everett switched the reins to his left hand, then he made as if to reach for the buckle of his belt but drew instead, and his shots clipped the guns from the other two riders. Everett's experience told him that Chance would never face Everett, one on one. In all their years of running together, Chance had never been as fast or as good a shot as Everett was. "Drop it, Chance," Everett told him.

"I can't, Everett." he said. "I'm the sheriff now."

"If you don't," Everett said, "Leavenworth will lose two sheriffs in less than a day, and this one will be on me. Now drop it."

Looking around, Chance saw the boys riding with him were still rubbing their hands from having the pistols shot from them. Chance looked at Everett with fire in his eyes. For a split second, Everett thought Chance was going to try it. Then, Chance let the pistol drop from his fingers. "You can't beat this, Everett," Chance said to him.

"When did I ever beat anything in that town?" Everett replied. "Boy, you're acting just like your pa, wanting to lock me up without even hearing my side of things. On my mother's grave, Chance, I did not kill your pa, but when I ride away from here, it's over. I will kill any man that follows me. This is over, do you hear me? Go back to town and look for the real killer, because it isn't me. Now ride, all of you."

They turned their horses and walked off a lot slower than they'd came up. *I guess I knocked the wind out of them a little,* Everett thought. He rode away thinking, or at least hoping, it was over. He'd been no great admirer of Sheriff Charlie Mason, but he knew he was not the killer.

He rode the sun down again before making his camp. Tonight would be a cold camp, just in case them boys got a wild hair and decided to come at him again, maybe this time with guns blazing before they lost their nerve. They did not show up, and he was glad of it.

*

Three weeks later, he rode into Denver without seeing any more of Chance or the other boys. The first night in Denver, he met an old man at the saloon they named Pick. He was a prospector, and he told Everett, he had found a little vein up in the hills. His trouble was, he was near about eighty years old and not able to really work the claim as it needed to be. His second problem was that he trusted nobody in town. They're were all either too lazy to work, or they would cut your throat for a plug nickel, in Pick's opinion.

Pick tried to cut Everett in as a full partner, if Everett would agree, or Pick would sell him the claim, straight out, for ten thousand dollars. "No, thanks." Everett told him. "I'm just back from hunting buffalo on the Texas plains. I was out there for three years. I've got a little money put aside, and until it's near gone, I'm not going to be looking for no work." Besides, Everett had nowhere near that much money. "All I want to do is ride the high country for a while, and take it easy," he told the old man. He told Pick, too, about being messed up by that bull.

Two days later, he rode out of Denver to do just what he'd said. He intended to ride these mountains over and maybe find him a little valley, hid someplace, where a man could live in peace and live off the land. Alone so much out there on the plains, he'd gotten real good at being alone. In fact he thought it to be good for the soul.

The reception he'd gotten back in Leavenworth had proven, once again, why he cared nothing for living among others anymore. *This is really a man's country out here*, he thought. One time, he just sat his horse and watched an eagle soaring high above for most of an hour. Another time, he came upon two bighorn sheep trying to settle a dispute, or maybe they were just sharpening their skills. Either way, after watching for a while, he rode on. He had food enough for now, but it was good to know they were here.

For the first time he could remember, he was in no hurry. He was not worn to distraction from working and was not worried about his next meal. He was a man of leisure, and it felt good. The fourth day up there in God's country, he came across exactly the kind of place he had hoped to find. It was high up, and as the trail started down, he saw a fairly large green valley far below him. A stream ran its course, starting at one side on the upper end, and angling across the valley by the time it reached the lower end. This stream he would investigate more closely. The trail down, if it really deserved the name of a trail, looked as though it had not been used in many years. He figured the last people in this valley were Indians, long ago. It was possible that he was the first white man ever to come into this valley. When he finally reached the bottom, the night was nearing dark, so he decided to make camp and look the valley over in the morning.

He started a small fire, then went to the stream to get water for coffee, taking Mouse along, so the horse could drink. He arrived at the stream, along with the last streaks of sunlight, and he startled a small herd of deer on the other side. It was good to know that there were deer in the valley. Some animals had far-reaching areas that they wandered, but deer stayed mostly within a few miles of where they were born. "Why wouldn't they?" he said himself. "It's perfect here."

He got back to the fire and set the coffee pot near the fire's edge. The weather was cool even this far down the peaks. Not cold, though, not yet anyway. He knew that would change in the coming months, and he would have to be better prepared for cool weather than he was right now.

As he sat that night, he decided to make a trip back into Denver and supply himself properly for the coming winter. Also, if he found no one in this valley tomorrow, this is where he would come back to. This would be his home.

Other than waking long enough to add a stick or two to the fire, he slept like a baby. He was up and having some bacon and coffee when the sun peeked over the edge of the summit and into the valley. For two days, he explored every nook and cranny, as his ma used to say, looking for any sign of human life. The only signs he found appeared to be several hundred years old. There were crumbling remains of housing built right into the cliff walls of the valley in a couple of places.

While looking into some of the lower houses that seemed safe enough, he had found pieces of pottery and a lot of chips where arrowheads had been made. Everett knew nothing of which Indian tribes had lived in this part of the world, and as long as they were no longer here, he didn't think much about it. Most of the houses were crumbling to the point of falling, and he thought them to be unsafe to enter. He found no humans, but he did see more of those bighorn sheep, and a couple of what he would later learn were elk. There were signs of a mountain lion too, but he would leave it alone, if it would leave him alone. When he stopped once to drink from the stream, he saw fish swimming in great schools.

At camp on the third night, he was convinced that he was truly alone here, and that was as he wished. The next day, he would leave for Denver to get his winter supplies. If he were able to go there and back quick enough, he would have time to build a decent shelter before the first snow came to the mountains. In the spring, he would start a cabin. Near the lower end of the valley there was a good stand of trees, some pine and some aspen, and there were deadfalls by the ton for firewood.

The man at the general store remembered him. Remembered his face anyway, for he had never told the man his name, and the store owner had never asked. This was the way of the West.

In the back of his mind, he still believed Chance

Mason would come looking for him at some point. If the situation had just involved a sheriff who was his boss that would have been one thing, but the sheriff had also been Chance's father, and that, Everett didn't think, Chance could let go of very easily. Not unless he had found out who had really killed Charlie Mason back in Leavenworth.

As he was adding up the total, the storekeeper asked if Everett was going prospecting. "No, sir," he told him, "I have found something better than gold."

"Better than gold!" exclaimed the storekeeper. "That would be sort of a hard thing to do."

"Not in my way of thinking," said Everett. "I found me a little valley up there that I intend to live in with just the peace and quiet."

"Not me," the storekeeper said. "I'm a city man myself. I like the hustle and bustle of people."

When the storekeeper had a total for his goods, Everett realized all the things he'd bought would be too much for Mouse to carry up those steep trails, once he factored in his own two hundred pounds. "Got any idea where a man might buy a packhorse or a mule?" he asked. He was sent to the livery stable and was soon back with a mule. He made a bundle of the supplies and packed them on the mule. Then he put together a smaller parcel and tied it behind his saddle.

"Well, good luck to you, friend," the store owner told him as he mounted. "I've heard winters can be mighty fierce up there."

*

Trailing the mule along behind, he returned to the valley. Just before reaching his camp, he saw a huge elk just standing there, completely unafraid. It was almost as if Everett was the first human the elk had ever seen, and that just might have been the case.

"May as well get started putting back some meat for the winter," he whispered to Mouse as he reached for his rifle. He cased out the small caliber rifle he'd just bought and brought down the elk. As he stood over the animal, Everett thanked the elk for its life that would help him keep his own through the winter.

He rode on the hundred yards or so to his camp,

unloaded the mule, and took the saddle off Mouse. Then, he picketed Mouse on some good grass, and led the mule with him to carry the meat back to camp after he finished butchering the elk. The skin he would keep too, as his moccasins were beginning to wear thin, and he knew it wouldn't be long before he would be needing new ones. The ones he now wore he had traded for, but the next pair he would have to make for himself.

It was evening before he finished his job with the elk, and as soon as he was back in camp, he built a fire and a crude drying rack. Most of the meat he would smoke-cure for winter, but the back strap he would have for his supper. While that was cooking, he made a few changes to his shelter. Then, he arranged the supplies he had just bought. The meat and anything that might attract animals, he put in a big sack that he would pull up into a tree for the night. The next day, he would cut some logs and build a safe place for the items in the sack on the ground near his shelter. Once the sun had gone down, the temperature grew colder, very quickly. He knew it wouldn't be long before cold weather, because winter would come early up this high.

Even though he was in a valley, he was still a long way up in these mountains. Over the next two months, he began getting as far from camp as possible to hunt, hoping to keep game closer when the snow prevented him from getting far from camp. He fished quite a bit and smoked a lot of the fish for his winter cache.

He awoke one morning to find a bright sun in the sky and the temperature fairly high, so he decided to make the ride into Denver, one more time, for coffee and a few other things he had forgotten on his last trip. There was only one way in and out of that valley that he had found, and it would not be passable with ice or snow on the ground.

At the general store, he quickly gathered what he needed, including a couple more blankets just for good measure. As he was about to leave, the store owner asked if his name happened to be Evers. "Matter of fact, it is," Everett told him.

"Fellow in here a couple of days ago looking for you," the storekeeper said.

"What did this man look like?" Everett asked.

"Smaller than you," the man said, "and his hair was darker, too."

"Did you tell him where I was?" Everett asked.

"Couldn't even if I'd wanted to," the storekeeper replied. "First off, I didn't even know you was Evers, and second, I don't have a clue where your place is located."

"Was he wearing a badge?" Everett asked.

"None that I could see," the man said. "The fellow said he was just an old friend from Kansas, was all."

"Thanks," Everett told him. "He used to be my friend, but you know how things can change. Listen, if he comes back in again, just tell him the same thing, okay?"

"Sure," the storekeeper said, "makes no difference to me one way or the other. Besides, you've bought a lot of supplies from me, and he didn't buy a thing."

"Thanks, again," Everett told him, then went out and rode home. He watched his backtrail until he started the climb up the peak. About a half-mile up from the valley floor, there was a spot where a person could look back down to the trail at the bottom. He had stopped there every time to look at his backtrail. "Damn," he said as a rider came into view.

He knew it was Chance Mason at once, and he wished Chance had left things alone like Everett had told him to. Chance was still about ten miles from where the switchback trail started up the mountain. *Well*, Everett thought to himself, *it'll be dark by the time he reaches the switchback. Maybe he will ride right past it in the dark.* If Chance tried this trail for the first time in the dark, he would wind up at the bottom somewhere. *Well*, thought Everett, *I'm sure not going to wait on him.*

From that point, it was still twenty miles to the trail leading down into his valley. He would have light for a little longer, going across the ridge, then he would have to take the trail down to his camp in the dark. As he rode over the ridge, he felt something hitting his face, and realized it was very light snow. As angry as he was with Chance right now, he hoped his childhood friend wouldn't try to follow him over the mountain, or Chance would surely die.

Everett knew the snow might quit soon, and then

again, it might last for days, or even weeks. The temperature had dropped surprisingly fast when the sun had left the sky. The trail down into the valley gave him a scare or two, but that surefooted little horse of his never slipped once. Still, he was a happy man when he rode into camp.

The first thing he did was to get a fire going and start some coffee. He was too tired and frazzled to cook, so he ate some jerked elk and drank a whole pot of coffee. He had built a lean-to for Mouse and the mule, off to the side of his own shelter, to keep the snow off of them and opened it toward the fire for heat. Looking up from beside the fire, Everett saw that the flakes had gotten bigger, and were coming down harder. He had opened the door to his own shelter to allow the heat to get in, as well. Once the fire burned down some, he would go in and close the makeshift door for the night.

When he awoke in the early morning hours, it was cold. Slipping on his boots and wearing only long johns, he went out to get a fire going. There was about six or eight inches of snow covering everything. He couldn't even see the stream. He looked in on Mouse and the mule, and they were both doing fine in their shelter.

Winter In Denver

By the time the fire was burning good and putting off some heat, Everett had gone in the shelter and dressed. Soon, the sun would be up, and the temperature would warm up a little, or so he hoped. Early on, he had found a large area of tall grass already turning brown and having no real tools to cut it with, he had just broken handfuls of it off close to the ground and piled it near the shed. Mouse and the mule sure seemed to appreciate his efforts. Of course, with no more snow than this, they could paw away the snow to get to the grass beneath. Everett decided he had better save the rest of the hay until the snow was such that the animals couldn't get grass for themselves.

As he was having a second cup of coffee, an idea crossed his mind concerning Chance. Chance was a grown man, Everett told himself. Everett would not risk going on the trail out of here and maybe get all broken up in a fall himself, to be sure a man he may have to kill later was okay. He hadn't asked Chance to come out here.

In fact, Everett had warned him not to follow.

As the sun climbed high in the sky and glistened off the snow, Everett thought nothing he had ever seen was as pretty as that little valley right then. He brought the animals out to let them find some fresh grass. He then spent part of the day adding a few branches here and there to his shelter and stopping up some holes the wind had shown him last night.

A little after noon, he took his rifle and walked out toward the far end of the valley. About five miles from camp, he saw a small herd of deer. They were downwind from him, so he decided to close in on them a little before making his shot. He had done a lot of long-distance shooting on the plains, but the rifle he now carried had nowhere near the takedown power of that .50-caliber. When Everett was about two hundred yards from the herd, he looked for the best shot. He moved the muzzle from target to target looking for the biggest one. While looking for the biggest deer in the herd, Everett spotted a big old black bear. The bear was filling up on some berries, or something, and was paying no attention to anything else.

The Indians of the plains preferred robes of buffalo hide for winter, but Everett had heard that the old mountain men who lived and trapped in these mountains years ago had worn bearskins. Since there were no buffalo around here, and the bear was, he won—or rather lost. Settling his rifle against his shoulder, Everett dropped the bear with a shot to the neck. Having never killed a bear, Everett was in no hurry to go check his kill. The shot echoed for what seemed like an hour off the walls of the valley. The deer had wandered off, but seemed in no big hurry, as if they knew Everett would be busy with the dead bear for a while. The fact was, the herd had probably never heard a gun fired and so had no fear of it. The buffalo had been that way, for the most part, when he first got to the plains in Texas. *Well,* he thought, *if Chance had come up the mountain and stayed last night, he sure knew now that I was here, or that someone was.*

*

Chance Mason hadn't heard the shot, since Denver was too far away. He had known a few days ago that it was Everett he was following, but he'd lost the trail. He had never been as good at tracking as Everett had been, when they were growing up. Then, as the snow started falling, Chance had found what he thought was the beginnings of a steep trail going up into the mountains, but he wasn't about to go up an unknown trail at dark, so he had turned back for Denver.

At the saloon, he talked to several men about the weather, since he was not familiar with the area. "It's an early one," an old man had told him. "Could be that this will blow over in a day or two and be fairly good weather for another month. Then again, I've seen it start this early and not let up much for a few of months."

"What are the odds of me getting into the mountains?" Chance asked the old man.

"You got a place up there?" he asked Chance.

"No," he said, "I'm looking for a man that's up there somewhere."

"If you don't have a cabin, a cave, or at least a really well- built shelter, I'd advise you to not go traipsing up there until spring," the old man told him. "It's real easy for a man to die up there, Son."

"Well, then, I guess I'll see what this weather does," said Chance.

"This man that you're looking for," responded the old man, "is he a friend, or are you a lawman?"

"I was a lawman," said Chance, "and yes he is, or at least was, a friend. If I can find him, maybe we can be friends again."

*

When Chance Mason and those other two men had ridden back to Leavenworth without Everett that day, the city elders called Chance in and told him they weren't sure if he was ready for the sheriff's job. "Three of you couldn't bring in one man," they had said. "He killed our sheriff, and your father."

Chance talked them into giving him a month, on the condition that if he didn't have Everett in jail or hadn't found out who had been responsible for the sheriff's death by the end of that month, he would step down from the job on his own.

Three weeks later, while making his nightly rounds, he bumped into Otis Cummins. Otis was staggering out of the saloon and ran right into Chance. "Watch where you're going, boy," said Otis. As he staggered off down the street, Chance wondered to himself where Otis had gotten the money to get so drunk. Chance decided to ask some questions, and the barkeep seemed the best place to start.

"In answer to that question," the barkeep had told him, "I "might have an idea where Otis got that money." He related that Otis had been spending quite a bit lately. "I thought maybe he had sold off some property or something," the barkeep said. "Then, last night he was very drunk, and I overheard him telling Matt Farley that he'd stolen the money from a hotel room. He was saying how that stupid kid didn't deserve the money."

"I have another question that maybe you can answer for me, Grady," said Chance.

Grady Wilkes said, "You know me, Chance. If I can help, I will."

"A couple of months back, a man came to town. He wore buckskins, head to toe. Do you remember him coming in the saloon?" Chance asked.

"Sure do," said Grady. "In fact, the first time he came in, Otis came in right behind him with a silver dollar. Then, after Otis had drunk two shots, he left, and the fellow you're asking about called me over and asked who Otis was. I told him the story that I'd heard about what happened to Otis. How some kid had made him lose everything."

"The man we're talking about was that kid," said Chance.

"Well, I had the feeling that Otis had hit him up for that dollar, before that man came in here," said Grady.

"Grady, how much do you think Otis has spent in here in the last few weeks?" asked Chance.

"I'd say close to eighty dollars," replied Grady. "He has left here every night plastered."

"Thanks," said Chance, "you may have just told me who really killed my pa. I'll see you later, Grady. I need to go do some thinking."

Sitting in the sheriff's office, Chance remembered back to how Otis Cummins had come blustering into the office that morning, telling his father how the Evers boy had caught him nearly drunk and beat and robbed him. He kept on complaining until the sheriff finally stood up and told Otis that he would go right then and arrest Evers. *My God,* he thought. *My father was as bullied by Cummins as everyone else around here.*

Chance remembered, how, after the trial, Otis and his father had a bad argument. Otis was yelling at his father that he didn't deserve to be sheriff for not making sure that kid stayed in jail. The idea hit Chance like a bolt of lightning that Everett had been telling him the truth. Otis had recognized him, then had robbed Everett's room. He must have taken the money and that bone handled knife. Then, he had snuck into his pa's house and stabbed him, while he slept. That was one enemy gone and the other one would be blamed and hanged for it. *That had to be what happened,* thought Chance. *I was so stupid. Everett Evers may have done a few things wrong, but I never knew of him to lie about any of it.*

The next day, Chance went to see Angie Washburn. "Angie," he said, "I need to ask you something and please tell me the truth, even if you think it may hurt me, okay?"

"What is it, Chance?" she replied. "You look so serious. Are you all right?"

"No, not really," he said. "Angie, when Everett came back to town, and the two of you went to supper that night, will you tell me what happened?"

She told him exactly what had happened. "I'm sorry, Chance, she said, "but I loved him so much before he left town, and I guess I was just weak when he came back. When we got to the house, I asked him to come in, but he refused, saying that he was a better friend than that. I can't tell you what might have happened if he had, because I don't know, but now I'm glad he didn't. Especially since he killed your pa and everything. I'm sorry to have acted that way. Can you ever forgive me?"

"I guess part of that was my fault, too," he told her. "He asked me to come along with you two that night, and I refused, because I was jealous." Chance told her what he had learned, and that it looked like Everett had not been the one that killed his pa, after all. "I still have to figure out how to get Otis to admit it, but I'm sure now that Otis is guilty."

"Chance," she said, "we were both very ugly to him, and he really never done a wrong thing to either of us."

"I know," said Chance, "and if I can get Cummins convicted of killing pa, I intend to set things right with Everett, if I can."

After he left Angie, he went and found Matt Farley. "Well," said Matt, "Otis never went into any real detail about what happened, just that he had broken into the room of that Evers boy and got back some of his own money. He also said that he wasn't finished with Evers. 'I aim to make him suffer as much as I have,' he said. 'Evers and the rest of them, too.' I didn't know Everett was back in town," said Matt. "Leastways, not until somebody told me that was him dressed in them buckskins."

"Would you swear, in court, to what Otis told you?" Chance asked.

"If it would get rid of that old drunk bully, you damned right I would!" exclaimed Matt.

"Thanks," said Chance. "I'll let you know when I need you, if I can bring it to that point."

*

It was a long day's ride to Topeka, but Chance wanted to talk to the judge in person, to tell the judge what he'd learned. Chance also wanted to know if the judge thought Otis Cummins could be convicted just on what other people had said. As far as Chance knew, no one had seen Cummins enter or leave his father's house.

The judge sat and listened as Chance explained all that had happened in Leavenworth concerning his father's death. "Those names sound familiar," said the judge.

"Yes, sir," said Chance. "Three years ago, or a little more, you handled a case where Cummins was accusing Evers of beating and robbing him. Turned out, it was a fair fight. Evers had only taken what was rightfully owed to him for work he'd done for Cummins."

"Yes, yes," said the judge. "I remember now. This Cummins man was something of a bully, and young Evers had whipped him after not being paid. As I recall, there was quite a few witnesses for young Evers."

"Yes, sir," said Chance. "That's right, and that's

because Evers is good man."

"Well, that gives Cummins motive for wanting to get back at the Evers boy, and with what you've just told me, to get revenge against your father as well. I'm surprised he didn't come after me, too," said the judge. "Go home, Sheriff, and arrest this man. I will be along in a few days to hold trial."

Two days later, Chance Mason went to the hovel that Otis Cummins called home. He went alone because he felt that he had something to prove to himself, if to no one else. Chance wanted to prove that he could handle the job as sheriff of Leavenworth, and that he could handle Otis. He knocked on the wall of the ramshackle building, and when Otis walked out, Chance said, "Otis Cummins, you are under arrest for the murder of Sheriff Charlie Mason."

"Go to hell," said Otis. "Your friend, Evers, did it, not me, but you were too yellow to bring him in."

"I was wrong in thinking that Everett did it at all," said Chance, "but this time I'm not. Now, are you going quietly?"

Cummins swung at him, but Chance was expecting it and laid the butt of his pistol against Otis' big head. Otis went to the ground hard, and by the time he had recovered his senses, he was handcuffed. Chance dragged him to his feet and marched him up Main Street to the jail. Before he even had Otis locked in the cell, some of the town elders had come in. "What's all this?" one of them asked Chance.

"I've arrested him for the murder of Sheriff Mason," said Chance.

"Son, when we told you to arrest the man who did it to prove you were capable of doing this job, we meant the right man," an elder stated.

"That's what I've done," Chance replied. "Now, gentlemen, if you don't mind, I have things to do. I have to wire the judge and set up with the barkeep to close the saloon for a trial when the judge gets here." With that said, he ushered them out the door and closed and locked it behind them.

Turning toward the cells, he said, "Cummins, if you want anything other than bread and water until the judge gets here, I don't want to hear nothing out of you."

Three days later, the judge arrived in Leavenworth, and a trial was set for the following day. That same day that the judge arrived in town, another witness came forward. Mr. Clarkson lived on the lot next to the sheriff's house, and he told Chance that he had seen something. "I heard a commotion at your father's house. Early in the morning he was found dead. When I first heard the sound of arguing, Chance, I thought it was you and your father, but when I realized it was somebody else, I looked out my window on that side of the house. As I was looking out, I saw a large man come from the back of the house and go toward the woods behind it," Clarkson reported.

"Could you see who it was, Mr. Clarkson?" asked Chance.

"I never saw a face," Clarkson said, "but I've seen Otis Cummins around town for enough years to know it was him."

"Why did you not come to me, right away?" Chance asked.

"Heck, Boy, I'm ashamed to say it, but until he was in jail, I was scared if he found out I said anything, he would kill me, too."

A week later, Otis Cummins had been found guilty and was hanged for the murder of Sheriff Charlie Mason. The day after the hanging, the city elders came to Chance and told him, as far as they were concerned, he was the new sheriff of Leavenworth, Kansas. "Thank you, gentlemen," he said, "but I'm afraid you will have to find somebody else. I have something more important that I must do right now."

Chance went to Angie's and told her he was leaving.

"What about us?" she asked him. "You said you could forgive me."

"I do forgive you, Angie," said Chance, "but right now, I'm going to look for Everett. If I can find him, I'll tell him how wrong I was and how wrong this whole town was about the kind of person he is."

"Are you coming back?" she asked him.

"I really don't know," he told her, "But because of that, I can't expect you to wait for me. Find yourself another man, and I wish you well."

He went to his own little house and packed what few things he would take with him. Then, he walked over to the sheriff's office, and taking the badge from his vest, placed it on the desk. "Sorry, Pa," he said, "but I just don't think I'm cut out for this." Pulling open the bottom drawer, he took out that large bone handled knife, and wrapped it in a cloth to be placed in his saddle bag.

Very early the next morning, he rode out of town toward the West. Five days later, he rode into Denver and started asking around about Everett Evers. Somehow Chance knew Everett was, or at least had been, in this town. The man at the store told Chance he didn't know the man he asked about, but for some reason Chance thought maybe he did.

As he was riding into town one day after chasing a lead, he caught a glimpse of a man he thought could be Everett. He followed the man for miles, but lost him in the dark and snowfall. Now, here he sat, waiting to see if the weather was going to clear up, or if he would have to wait until spring to find out if the man he'd followed was, in fact, Everett Evers. It was a good thing Chance had never been much of a drinker and had never gambled. He had managed to put back almost all the money he had ever made. *If I have to sit in this town until spring, I will need every penny,* Chance thought.

One night, at the saloon, he was having a beer, and he started talking to an old man who sat beside him. "Sure thing," said the old man, "I saw him and talked to him. Fact is, I tried to get him to come in with me on a little claim I have."

"Gold?" asked Chance.

"What else is there?" the man asked him.

From down the bar, came a voice that said, "You know, I asked a fellow that same question not long back, and he told me he had found something better up in the mountains. He said it was even better than gold. I told him that I'd sure like to know what that was," said the voice. "According to him, it was a little valley he found, and he was planning to live there in the peace and quiet. He said he had a run-in with a buffalo bull some time back, and he had some problem with a friend of his. In my opinion, he is plumb soured on people, that one is. I'd also venture to say he is a man best left alone."

"He'd better have a good shelter, is all I know," said the old man.

"Say, young man, how about you?" the old man asked.

"How about me what?" asked Chance.

"How would you like to own half of a gold mine?"

"I really don't think I'm the man you need, old timer. I hate to admit it, but I've really never been too much for hard labor," replied Chance.

"What is your line of business?" he asked Chance.

"Well, my pa was the sheriff in Leavenworth, and for a while I was his deputy," Chance responded.

*

Three days later, the snow was mostly gone. Chance bought some things and packed his horse for a trip. "You going up there looking for him?" the store owner asked.

"Yes, sir," Chance told the storekeeper. "I have to find him."

"I heard a little from you in the saloon the other night, and I've heard a little from him. Evers, I mean," said the storekeeper.

"You do know him then," stated Chance.

"No," the man replied, "not really. He just showed up a time or two, buying supplies."

"You said, the other night, that he had found himself a valley up there. Do you know where?" asked Chance.

"Are you hunting him for some crime, or something?" he asked Chance.

Chance told him the whole story about what had happened in Leavenworth. "Now," he said, "I just want a chance to say I was wrong."

"Son, I honestly have no idea where his place is, but you be careful up there. His is not the only valley in them mountains, and a man new to them can get almighty turned around up there. Keep in mind, too, that you know you're no longer the law, but he don't know that. I will tell you this, when he was last here, he supplied up pretty hard. He don't plan to be back for a long time, or maybe never," said the storekeeper.

"Thanks," said Chance. "I'll go careful, but I have to go." He rode out of Denver and back to where he had lost the trail that evening. He camped the first night at the foot of the switchback trail. In the morning, he would go up into that monstrous mass of peaks and valleys in search of his old friend.

*

His axe bit deep into the tree with each swing of his powerful arms. Everett had awakened early, like always, and the sky was clear. *Maybe,* he thought, *I'll get a while longer before the real snows falls.* In the meantime, Everett had decided to start felling some trees that he would need in the spring. He knew he'd not have time to build his cabin, but at least this would be a start and keep him active.

His shelter required little work now, and he had a good supply of meat and other things laid in and a huge pile of hay for his stock. When winter really started, he believed he would be prepared. At least, as much as a man can be prepared for what nature threw at him.

He tried not to, but he did wonder at times about

what had become of Chance. Everett had ridden the trail out as far as the overlook, where he had seen Chance in the valley below. Maybe he had looked up at those mountains and decided that he would never find Everett up there and had returned home.

By evening, Everett had cut down and cleaned up what he thought would be a good start on the logs he would need in the spring. As he crossed the stream, he stopped and had a drink from the cold clear water. This stream ran through his valley, his home.

Everett had never known his father. It had always been just him and his ma. He faintly remembered moving around a lot, from one rented place to another, before coming to Leavenworth. For a time, he had thought of Leavenworth as his home, but even there, the land and the house they lived in belonged to somebody else. This valley, though, was his. He had decided to file a mining claim for this valley in the spring, although he had no intentions of doing any mining. Still, it would keep others from trying to mine in the valley.

*

The trail under his horse's hooves was solid rock, so Chance knew looking for tracks was a waste of time. He had known men who could track across almost anything. Everett was one that could, but not Chance. All he could do was ride and watch for trails leading off the main trail going down into the valley. If he got lucky, he might see smoke from a cook fire. He rode each evening until almost dark, looking for just that.

On his third day, he was watching an eagle soaring overhead, and as his eyes followed it back in the direction from which he had come, and he saw smoke. He waited a full minute, afraid to move his head for fear of losing the spot, until he was sure he really saw what he thought he did. Chance saw it again; a thin trail of smoke rising to the clouds. *I must have missed a turnoff somewhere,* he thought. *Rode right past it even though I was watching closely.*

Of course, seeing smoke didn't mean he had found Everett. It only meant that he'd found somebody. The thought of Indians crossed his mind, and he realized he wasn't even sure if there were any Indians in these mountains. Now, he had to worry about being shot by

Everett, if indeed, that's who he had found. After all, that morning outside of Leavenworth Everett had said he would kill anybody that followed him. It could be the fire of some old prospector, itchy about anyone coming near his claim, and now he had the thought of possible Indians. Chance had not thought about any of those things before riding up here.

Suddenly, he saw the trail going down into the valley where he had spotted the smoke. The trail was clearly visible when riding in this direction. Not knowing how far down the trail would take him, he decided it would be best to camp right there at the head of the trail for the night. He set about finding wood for a fire.

*

Everett looked at the top again and thought to himself, *it definitely is a fire up there. It has to be Chance.* It sure wasn't a local man camping on top of the crest in all this wind, then building a fire big enough that anybody could see it for miles around. He would be ready for Chance in the morning. Everett had no desire to kill Chance Mason. They had been friends for many years, but he would not go back to Kansas alive. If that was what Chance had in mind, one of them would die here tomorrow. He finished his coffee and put out his fire for the night.

Everett was up before sunrise, as usual, and for the first time since coming to the mountains, he strapped on his gun belt. Sliding the pistol from the holster, he dumped the shells into his hand. He wiped each one free of dust and reloaded the gun. He would not hide, or even be inside, when Chance came to the camp. Everett would be standing out front to meet him. Until then, he would drink his coffee as he did every morning. Just before ten o'clock, Everett could hear the footfalls of a horse on the hard rock trail.

Before coming into view, Chance shouted, "Is this the camp of Everett Evers?"

"It is," said Everett. "Come on in, Chance, but come in with your hands empty."

Chance Mason rode to within twenty feet of the shelter and stopped. "Thanks for not shooting me," he said.

"The day's not over yet," Everett told him. "I'm not going back to Leavenworth, Chance, it's just that simple. If that's why you're here, pull that hog leg and let's get this over with."

"Everett," said Chance, "I'm not wearing a badge, and if you'll let me, I'll drop my gun belt. I just need to talk to you."

"Climb down," Everett told him. When he was standing beside his horse, Chance reached to unbuckle his belt. "Leave it." said Everett. "You could never beat me anyway. Coffee?" he asked, purposely turning his back on Chance.

"Sounds good," said Chance, walking on to the fireside. "Man, I thought I would freeze up there last night. I camped at the top of your trail."

"I know," said Everett, "and I knew it was you. Nobody who lives in these mountains would camp up there in the wind and then build a bonfire."

"You knew it was me?" asked Chance. Everett nodded. "Everett, look, I'm here to tell you, I was wrong. I should have known and trusted you when you told me you didn't kill Pa. I was wrong for the way I treated you, and so was a lot of other people in town."

"Did you find the killer?" he asked Chance.

"Otis Cummins," said Chance.

"Otis!" exclaimed Everett. "Why would he kill the sheriff?"

"He blamed you for all his hard times after you whipped him that night," said Chance, "then, he bullied Pa into arresting you. In court, you beat him again, and he blamed Pa for that, too. He stole your money, and this," said Chance pulling the bone handled knife from behind him. "He killed Pa with this, knowing people had seen you wearing it, and that they would blame you. Knowing the history between you and Pa, just made it easier for Otis. He was right, too. I'm sorry to say this, but I'm one of the ones that believed you were guilty."

"How did he get caught?" asked Everett.

"He couldn't leave the booze alone and started spending your money, getting drunk every night and talking too much."

"Have you arrested him yet?" asked Everett.

"We arrested him, tried him, and hung him," said Chance, "then, I turned in my badge."

"Why?" asked Everett. "It appears you're pretty good at being a sheriff."

"No, I'm not," said Chance. "If I was any good at it, I would have known you were telling the truth on the road that day." He handed the knife to Everett and said, "I really am sorry, Everett. I also want to apologize for the way I acted about Angie. You were right up front with me about seeing her on the street, and then like some stupid, jealous schoolboy, I told you I was too busy to go to supper with the two of you."

"Look, Chance, all that happened that evening was that we had supper, and then I walked her to her house," said Everett.

"I know," Chance replied. "She told me that and said she had invited you in, but you told her I was too good of a friend. I wish I'd been that kind of friend to you."

"Okay," said Everett, holding out his hand to shake. "What do you say we call it all forgotten?"

"I'd be glad to, if you can," said Chance. They sat by the fire and talked, just like they had done back when they were growing up. "You really like it up here, don't you?" Chance asked.

"No," said Everett, "I love it here. Just look around and tell me you don't. There's game aplenty, fish in the stream, and years-worth of firewood just laying around for the gathering. In the spring, I aim to build me a cabin across the stream, here in the lower end. Then, I'll have everything I need."

"What about people?" asked Chance.

"I've never been too good with them, anyway," said Everett. "I think we'll both get along without the other."

"Do you plan to hunt for gold?" Chance asked.

"I have no need to," Everett told him. "I have money enough from my hunting days to last me for years with no more than I need. What about you? Are you going back to Kansas, maybe marry Angie, and get that sheriff's job back?"

"I don't think so," Chance said. "Truthfully, I think she only took up with me because you were gone, and I'd gone to work for Pa and had a regular payday to spend on her."

"Plenty of room right here," said Everett.

"Thanks," Chance replied, "but this is not for me. I do need people around. No, I think I might go out to California. I'd like to see some new land for a change. Remember, I was born right there in Leavenworth, and this is as far as I've ever been from there. I have known everyone in town there, all my life. I think it's time I met some new people."

"You set for money?" Everett asked.

"I've got enough," he said. "I didn't spend it all on Angie Washburn. Besides, you need money to live on too, you know."

"Very little," said Everett. "Most everything I need this valley will provide to me."

Two days later they parted ways again, only this time it was as friends, and with a promise from Chance that if he came back this way sometime, he would look in on Everett. As he watched his childhood friend ride away, Everett thought, *how strange it is that two boys raised up the same way in the same small town should turn out so different.* "Good luck be with you, my friend," he said aloud. Then he turned to go into his shelter.

*

That first winter in the valley was as Everett figured it would be—hard, but not unbearable, to someone like himself that was used to a lot work. The worst of it had been a stretch of about two weeks, when he literally had to tunnel through the snow just to reach the animal shelter.

Mouse, and the mule, which he'd named Spook, sure seemed to appreciate his efforts. He had named the mule that because it was the easiest animal to scare that he'd ever seen in his life. His beautiful green valley was now completely covered in a blanket of white snow, and at times, there were rumblings from the upper peaks that he halfway feared would bring it all crashing down on top of him. Some days he left his shelter only long enough to feed the animals.

On better days, he would go hunting. He had made his last pair of buckskin boots larger than usual, then lined them with the fur from that ol' bear he had killed just before winter set in. He had also fashioned himself some snowshoes. Without them, it was dangerous, as he had found out one day when he was walking along, and the next thing he knew he was neck deep in a snow drift.

Eventually, spring started to creep in. He first noticed the sunshine seeming brighter, and then the snow started to melt in all but the shadiest of places. It would be months, he knew, before the snow was gone from the upper peaks.

One morning, he went to the stream for water for both his coffee and the animals. When he bent low to fill his coffee pot, the sun glinted off something on the bottom of the streambed. Reaching in the icy water, he brought up a handful of pebbles and among them were four small nuggets of gold. He tossed them back into the stream. It was good to know the gold was there, but for now at least, he didn't need it, and didn't want the attention it would bring to his valley. He went back to camp, watered Mouse and Spook, and made his coffee.

*

Two days after finding the gold, he woke up to a warm sunny sky and decided to ride into Denver. There was a big commotion going on as he came into town. The old man who had offered him a partnership in his claim had hit a big strike somewhere north of his valley.

I guess he found himself a partner, after all, thought Everett. He rode straight to the claims office to stake his own claim on the valley, before this new discovery set hundreds of men to hunting every inch of the mountains for their own strike. The valley was roughly twenty miles long but only about four miles wide at its widest point. He filed two claims; a mining claim at the upper end, and a homestead claim at the lower end, where he would build his cabin. The claims agent said he'd never had anybody file a homestead on land in the mountains, but since Everett was also filing a mining claim, he would do it. Between the two claims, the whole valley would be Everett's, legal and proper. He paid the man two dollars and was given papers to show ownership.

Everett knew there was gold in the stream, and he knew those nuggets he'd picked out of the stream were rough-edged. That meant the nuggets hadn't tumbled along very far down that stream, otherwise the edges would have been worn smooth. The source of those nuggets, and likely a lot more, could probably be found right at the head of the valley, somewhere. *The source can stay right where it's at*, he thought. If a time came that he needed it that would be different, but for now at least, he would not disrupt his valley with mining.

After leaving the land office, he went to the general store. "Evers," said the storekeeper when he walked in, "I see you made it through the winter."

"I did," said Everett, "but I don't think it was a really hard one this year. I think a wisdom greater than ours figured I needed to be broke in slowly."

"Maybe," said the storekeeper, "but I have a feeling you could handle about anything. What can I help you with today?"

Everett handed him the list of goods he'd made before leaving home. "Looks like you're getting ready to build a cabin," the storekeeper remarked.

"Soon as I get back," Everett told him.

"I guess you heard about old Gus hitting it big?"

"I'm happy for him," Everett said.

"You're still not planning to mine at your place?" asked John Pate, the owner of the store.

"No, sir," said Everett. "As I told you, I like it just fine the way it is."

"Evers, listen, about that young fellow that said he was a friend of yours—have you seen him?" asked Mr. Pate.

"I did," said Everett, "and we got things squared away between us. He's gone on to California to make a new life for himself."

"Well, just so you know, nobody in town really told him nothing, until after he told us what had happened back in Kansas. He said that he was only looking for you to apologize for the way he'd acted. Otherwise, we never would have told him anything."

"It's all right," Everett told him. "I'm just glad he caught the right man, that's all." When he had the mule packed, he headed back to the valley. As he neared the trail that turned down to his valley, he saw smoke. He knew somebody was at his shelter, because he had left no fire going. He went down the trail with his rifle across the saddle in front of him. His pistol was also ready for action, though still in the holster.

There was no such thing as approaching his camp quietly. The trail was merely a rock ledge, and a shod horse coming down it could be heard all over the valley. Everett decided to let Mouse trail in by himself, and he would follow behind. He heard a voice speak to the horse as it went into camp, and he thought his mind was surely playing tricks on him. *What in the world would a woman be doing up in these hills alone?* he thought. It dawned on him then that she wasn't alone. When Mouse went into camp, only the woman spoke, knowing a man would be coming behind him. Her man would be hidden somewhere waiting for Everett to come in. *Well,* he thought, *there's nothing to do but go on in.* This was his camp and his valley, and he'd be damned if they would have it without a fight. Now, he wasn't what you'd call good with a rifle lefthanded, but at close range he guessed it would be good enough. Gripping the rifle by the stock, pistol-like, he filled his right hand with his pistol and edging Spook forward, he walked on in.

As he came into camp, she stood up from beside the fire. "Howdy," she said, "did your horse throw you or something?"

"No, ma'am," he said, "I was just being cautious. Wasn't sure who was here or how many."

"It's just me," she said, holding out her hand to shake.

"Well, ma'am," he said, "I'll be glad to shake your hand, just as soon as you call your man to come in where I can see him."

"Honest to God, mister, there ain't nobody here but me. My name is Sue Bolen. I live with my pa two valleys over from here.

Dark was coming on, and I knew I'd never get home before it caught me. Pa and me, a couple of weeks ago saw that somebody had moved into this valley, so I thought, well, maybe I can stay here for the night."

Everett was beginning to relax a little bit by now. "Well, ma'am, I don't believe that would look very good, for a lady alone to stay here with a single man like myself," he said.

"In the first place," she said, "if you're worried about what that bunch in Denver would think, don't be. I've been tracking around these mountains with my pa longer than most of them have been there. Don't none of them think me no lady anyhow, but I thank you for saying it. If it was something else you was thinking though," she said, drawing a large knife from her side, "I can handle the likes of you."

"Yes, ma'am," he said, "I believe you could at that. Well, if you'll allow me to get my things from the shelter, I'll sleep right here by the fire, and you can sleep in there."

"Ain't no need to upset the applecart, as pa says. You just stay in there, and I'll sleep right here by the fire. I'll probably be gone long before you get up, anyway," said the woman.

"Have you eaten?" he asked her.

"Earlier today," said Sue. "I didn't want to lose no time since."

"Well, neither have I," said Everett. "So, why don't I cook up something?" They both relaxed and put down their weapons. Sticking out his hand, Everett told her his name and they shook.

He put together a stew with some elk meat and a few wild tubers he'd found growing near the stream. After their meal, they had some coffee, and she told him about herself and her pa. She said they had been up here prospecting for nearly eight years. They had found a little gold here and there, some from digs and some from panning. "It weren't enough to do more than keep body and soul together," said Sue. "You had any luck here?"

"Oh, I'm not prospecting," he told her.

"Not prospecting?" she said. "Then, why are you up here in the mountains?"

"I filed a claim on the upper end for prospecting and a homestead claim for the lower half here," Everett explained.

"You mean you claiming this whole valley?" Sue asked.

"Yes, ma'am," he said. "I aim to start me a cabin pretty soon and live right here from now on."

"But how will you know if there's gold here or not?" she asked.

"I don't care if there is or not," he told her. "I wish to live here for the beauty of the valley and the solitude it gives me."

"Running from the law, are you?" she asked.

"No," he told her, "It's nothing like that. I guess I'm just fed up with people."

"Most I've met are easy to get fed up with," she said.

True to her word, she was gone when Everett woke up about five the next morning. As he fixed some coffee, he thought about her. *It is one thing for a man like me to get fed up and wander around the hills*, he thought, *but not a woman*. She was that, sure enough, although a little rougher-edged than most he'd ever met.

*

The next month, he spent all day, most every day, working on his cabin. One day out of seven, he rested some and did his hunting. During that time, he noticed that his valley ran almost perfectly in an east-to-west direction. The valley got morning sun from the time the sun cleared the peaks, until the evening sun set behind them on the west end. That was the spot where his cabin would set. Between himself, Mouse, and the mule, they managed to move every log into place and soon the walls were standing. When he was about to start the roof, an idea struck him. By letting the rafter poles run long on one side, he could build a shelter for the animals under it with very little extra work. He made the roof very steep-pitched to help shed the snow, so as not to get so much weight on it. Folks in the lowlands would never believe how heavy snow was when it built up on a roof.

By the second week of May, the cabin was nearly completed. The fireplace rock he had gathered near the base of the mountains, and by using a stone boat he'd fashioned, he hauled them to the cabin site. He backed the fireplace up to the shed side, as he knew the heat from the rocks would help knock the cold off of it. As hard as Mouse and Spook had both worked lately, he figured they deserved a nice warm place in the winter, too. Although pine burned too quickly to be used alone, the drops from the wall logs he would not let go to waste.

When it was finished, the cabin was twenty-five-feet square with a ten-foot porch running the width of the front. There was also a sleeping loft in one end. His next project was building a small bridge over the stream, since the cabin sat on the opposite side of where the trail came into the valley. Once he had that completed, if there was time, he intended to build a smokehouse to better cure his meat. The smokehouse would also protect the meat from animals. He had seen the tracks of a mountain lion or cougar. Everett was not sure what they were called here. He had seen no sign of bear lately but was sure he had not killed the only one in the whole valley.

While working on the bridge one day, he saw two riders come into camp, and picking up his rifle, he went across to see who it might be. It turned out to be Sue Bolen and her pa. Her pa said his name was Samuel, and Everett told him his name. "Came by to thank you for letting Sue stay," Samuel said. "She handles a horse as well as any man, I reckon, but a father worries just the same."

"I see you wasted no time, Mr. Evers," she said, pointing across at the cabin.

"No, ma'am," he said, "I've been told the summers are short this high, so I aim to be ready for winter when it's ready for me."

"Looks like quiet a cabin," said Samuel. "Do you mind if I take a closer look?"

"Not at all," Everett answered, and the three of them walked to the cabin. Samuel took notice of how the logs fit, and how Everett had brought that long roof down.

"You a builder back in civilization?" Samuel asked.

"Done a little," Everett said, "among other things. Hunted buffalo for a while down on the plains in Texas."

"Yeah," said Samuel, "we did a little of that ourselves."

"We?" Everett asked him.

"Well, Sue and me," he said. "That gal is the best rifle shot you ever saw."

"I noticed she went well-heeled," Everett told him.

"Not her fault," Samuel said. "Her ma caught the fever and died when she was just a crawling baby. I did the best I could by her, but what did I know about raising a girl up to be a lady?"

"I was finding no fault, sir," said Everett. "Fact is, it's kind of nice to see a woman that can take care of herself. So many of them expect a man to fuss over them something awful."

"Not that one," Samuel replied. "I could not have had a son I'd trust more to have my back in any situation." Just then, Sue came back in the room. She had been out looking at the shed he'd built for Mouse and Spook.

"You done a real good job, Mr. Evers," she said.

"Well, thanks," he told her, "And please call me Everett."

"Well, we best be getting on, Pa, if we're going to make town before dark."

"Yep, you're right, Sue girl, and I sure am looking forward to it," said Samuel.

"Really?" asked Everett. "I took it you didn't like town much."

"Aw, that's Sue," Samuel said. "She's the one would just as soon stay in these mountains every day. I've got no hankering to live in town or nothing like that, but I do like to visit once in a while. They ain't no crime in having a drink and flirting with the girls."

Everett waved as they headed up the trail, then he went back to work on his bridge.

*

By July's end, he had finished the cabin, the bridge, and his log smokehouse. Even a bear would have to be powerful serious to get in that thing. The Bolens had come by once more, and Sue told him she had talked to her pa, and they had filed a claim on their valley as he had done. They had taken some ore into town with them, and it looked promising, so they was going to continue with their dig.

"Smart idea," Everett told her. "Filing a claim will keep other folks off what is yours."

"Don't you believe it," she said. "Right here is the only thing that can do that," she told him, lifting her rifle. "That claim just says nobody should get on it, is all." Well, he couldn't argue with logic like that, especially if they were to make a strike. The fact was, if they wanted gold, there would be folks crawling all over these mountains, and it wouldn't be people who cared if you had a legal claim or not.

So with that line of thinking, he rode to Denver for another rifle and more cartridges. "Better to have and not need, than to need and not have," he told John Pate. While he was there, he bought coffee and other supplies, as needed.

"You about to get settled in up there?" John asked him. Everett told him all he'd done, and that he was home.

"Had no run on picks or pans, have you?" he asked John.

"No. Why, you heard something?" John asked.

"No," said Everett, just checking to see if you had."

Once he was back in the valley, he relaxed and sat a long time over coffee, trying to decide what furniture he needed to build. A table for the kitchen and a couple of chairs were absolutely necessary. As for a bed, Everett would just as soon stay in his blankets on the floor. *A man can sleep way too sound in a big old comfortable bed, allowing all manner of things to happen to him,* he thought. Thinking back to his childhood in Kansas, he suddenly thought about Ma and how she had loved her porch swing. "Yes, sir," he said aloud, "I'll have one for myself." By the end of two days, there was one hanging on the porch of his cabin.

Greed In the Mountains

By mid-August, the temperatures had dropped to cool days and some very cold nights. Everett spent every day out hunting, starting at the far end of the valley, of course. He would ride Mouse part way there and walk the rest. The first day out, he got two big buck deer. *This may not take as long as I'd figured,* he thought as he cleaned and cut the meat. The second day, he saw several of those big old mountain sheep, high up on the side of a peak that he was sure no man could climb. *Just as well,* he thought. *Those old boys are probably nothing but muscle and bone.* They would be so tough; they'd have to be made into sausage before a man could chew the meat.

He was almost ready to accept defeat for the day, when he saw a huge bull moose. This thing was far taller than Mouse and must have weighed over a thousand pounds. Just about then, he was wishing he'd brought Spook along to help out with the hauling. Working his way around on the peak, he found the best possible shot. He'd brought the new rifle with him this time and was glad it was a bigger bore rifle than his other one. It still was not a big .50, like he'd used on the buffalo plains, but a .40-caliber. He had moved up to within a hundred yards of the moose and found a good position to shoot from. His first shot could not have been a miss, but you would have thought so.

The moose lifted his head and just stood there. Everett was somewhat surprised, but not really. He'd shot a few buffalo with that .50-caliber that had done the same thing. He was ready for a second shot, but he waited. When the moose started to walk away, he took two steps, and then his front legs just folded under him, and the moose went to the ground. Everett had known buffalo pretty well and still had managed to get himself hooked by one. As he'd never killed a moose before, he decided being cautious was the best way. While they weren't the sharp, curved horns of the buffalo, this thing had a set of antlers that spread four feet wide and nearly that high. The moose lay unmoving, but as cold as it was, Everett could see each breath the moose took. Finally, when the moose took no more breaths, he approached it. The moose was dead. Dropping down, he patted the moose on the shoulder and thanked it for giving its life to better his own.

He first walked back down to bring Mouse up to the kill, and then started the skinning. He had watched them old boys skinning and butchering the buffalo and had learned the best and fastest way to do both. By the time he finished, it was nearing dark. "Looks like we're here for the night," he told Mouse. "We can't pack all of this out at one time anyway, and I'm not about to leave it for wolves or bears." He had made up three packs of meat using the hide that he figured to weigh about two hundred-plus pounds each. If there had been trees big enough and close enough, he would have pulled up the meat into the branches, leaving it there but out of reach of animals until morning. Since there were no trees big enough, he quickly gathered some wood and got a fire going. Then, he stripped the saddle off Mouse, and tied him in a spot with a little grass.

Opening one of the packs at one end, he took out a good sized piece of backstrap, or, as some folks called it, tenderloin. Supper would be fresh moose tonight. From the saddlebag, he took his pot and some coffee that he always packed along. After a short walk to the stream for water, his supper was underway. Everett had dragged the carcass of that moose away from his camp, when he had gone to the stream. Later, after he'd finished supper and lay in his blankets, he was glad he'd done so. He was not sure just what they were, whether wolves or coyotes, but there was a lot of growling and fighting that went on over what remained of that moose.

By the light of morning, he loaded two packs on Mouse and one on his own back. He took the reins in hand, and they headed for home. Twenty miles was not much of a walk normally, but with a couple of hundred pounds on your back it was tough. It was a good feeling to see that cabin come into view. He cut the meat he'd just brought in and put it on the racks inside the smokehouse right away. By late evening, it was a terribly cold again, with a stinging sleet pushed by hard winds.

The winds came from the northeast and blew down that valley like a charging beast.

As he sat that night in his warm cabin over a cup of coffee, he thought of his friend, Chance, and wondered how he fared in California. If, in fact, he'd even made it there. He wondered, too, how Sue and her father were doing, and if their valley laid in the direction of his own. If theirs laid differently than his, the winds may pass high above them without their even knowing.

By morning, the wind was gone, and a warm sun once again hung in the sky. It was considerably warmer than the last few days and that concerned him. He'd heard stories about a warm spell this time of the year, meaning there was a fierce winter headed to the mountains. As it was warmer though, he put hunting on hold and used the day for Spook and himself to gather more of the deadfall trees closer to the cabin and to cut more of the high dried grass for use in the coming months. During his work, he decided that if this weather held on until the next day, he would ride in search of the Bolens' valley. *I am as prepared as possible,* he thought, and would go see if his neighbors needed any help.

During the night there was a rain storm. When he awoke the next morning, it was bitter cold again, and a light snow was falling from time to time. Walking outside, he quickly discovered that the rain from the previous night had formed thick ice on the ground, and he knew if this snow kept falling, nobody would be going anywhere from up here in the mountains.

The trail out would already be impassable from the ice alone. Although he had a lot of meat and fish he had smoked for the winter on hand, he still went hunting that evening. He walked out about a half mile on foot, afraid to put the animals on the icy ground. They were both very much needed for transportation, and Mouse had also been a trusted friend for a number of years. Everett would not take the chance of one of them breaking a leg. The abundance of game he saw put a fear in him. He knew that animals sensed things about the weather that man did not, or could not, and would feed heavy when a big storm was coming so the animals could lay up and wait it out. If that was the case, he was in for a bad one this winter. He took only a small young buck that day, hoping to not regret it later. This young buck he would not smoke but keep fresh and frozen for the few days it would last.

For the following three days, it was cold but with sunshine, and the ice melted away from the trail out. The second day, he took Mouse and Spook and went far up the valley almost to its end. There, he set up camp and leaving his animals there, he hunted. Everett had just approached small herd of deer and was lining up for a shot, when he heard a gun fire, only it wasn't his own. He'd not pulled the trigger. It wasn't in the valley but was close enough that it startled the deer he'd been watching, and they lit out down the valley back toward the cabin. As he stood up to go back to camp, he heard several more shots. The way they echoed; it was hard to say where they had come from.

He managed to kill a doe on the way to the cabin, so the day wasn't a complete loss. As he sat over a cup of coffee that evening, he wondered about those shots. Suppose there was another valley separated from his only by that ridge at the upper end? If someone was hunting that same end, that could explain the shots he'd heard. It wouldn't be the Bolens, though. They had both told him they were two valleys over from him. *It's a lot of mountain*, he told himself, *and not just you and the Bolens live up here.* Probably there was some old prospector holed up there a day or two to hunt, then he would move on.

By morning, there was six inches of snow on the ground, and the snow was still falling. *Okay,* he thought, *winter is here, like it or not, Everett.* For two days, he left the cabin only to throw a little hay to Mouse and Spook, then he came right back inside and sat by the fire. It was cold, a mean, bitter cold, and now there was at least ten inches of snow on the ground. This was what he had prepared for all year by his building this cabin, and the hunting and fishing he'd done. Now he could ride out the worst of it with relative ease. The fourth night, after the snow had started, he went on the porch for an armload of firewood, and as he was looking around, something caught his eye. At the far end of the valley, he could plainly see a small dot of light. Somebody had a fire going in his valley.

Wiping his eyes clear, he looked again, and it was still there. He went back inside and closed the door. The next day, if it wasn't snowing as hard, he would have to go up the valley and check it out. Laying two good sized hardwood logs on the fire, he thought, *but that's for tomorrow.* For now, he was going to have one more cup of coffee and go to bed.

Everett watched the morning light creep over the peak at the far end of the valley. No sun was visible, and there was only a lightness to the sky. He had breakfast and then dressed warmly. He had made some snowshoes weeks back and was yet to try them out. He'd never made any like these before, and he hoped they would work well. They were not the normal circular bearpaw shoes. These were made from the branches of a willow tree that grew near the stream. The outer ring branches were as big as his thumb and roughly five feet long. He'd not made a hoop of them but rather elongated them and tied the branches side-to-side in the back. Then, using some strips of hide and smaller branches, Everett had laced the bottom in a mesh. Directly where his foot would go, he stitched a pad of the moose hide, and strips of the same, to bind them to his feet. When they were tied on, he slung his rifle over his back along with a small pack of food. He added some tinder for a fire in case he got caught out there and couldn't get back to the cabin by nightfall. Then, he set out to see who was in his valley.

It was a long trek to the other end even with the shoes. They worked very well, but any snowshoe was cumbersome. The depth of the snow was only a matter of inches in places, but in others, it was closer to two feet. As he drew near where he thought he'd seen the fire, he slowed down and approached the place very carefully. He saw no fire now, but there was a faint smell of smoke hanging in the air. As he came to the burnt-out fire, he saw a body curled up, lying as close as could be to the embers. The person was also lying partly under a low bush, he supposed to keep the falling snow off them. Everett spoke but there was no answer, and he feared the person was dead from last night's cold weather. He called out again, only louder this time, and there was a stirring in the blanket. "Are you all right?" he asked.

A voice came back to him that sounded as though the person speaking was freezing, and he recognized the voice of Sue Bolen. Going to her and rolling her over to face him, he saw there was dried blood streaked down her face. Leaving her covered, he quickly got a rather large fire built up. He helped her sit up near the fire with the blanket over her shoulders. Then, he put on coffee from his pack. The coffee would do as much to warm her as the fire would. After she held a cup in her hand and had drunk a little, Everett asked her what had happened, and how she had gotten where she was. "They attacked us, and killed Pa," she said.

"Who did, Sue?" he asked her.

"They killed Pa," she said again, "and he thought they were his friends."

"Sue, how did you get here?" Everett asked.

"Where am I?" she inquired, looking over at him, but he didn't think she recognized him. *She will not survive another night outside,* he thought. Getting up, he began searching for two slender trees with which to build a travois in order to get her to the cabin. It had taken him the better part of five hours to get here. Of course, not knowing who was here, he had moved slowly. It would be dark, but barring the start of heavy snowing, he would get them back to the warmth of the cabin tonight.

When he had the travois ready, he told her what she needed to do. He helped her to lie down on the travois, and he covered her with her blanket and his from the pack. Once again putting his snowshoes on, he lifted the poles underneath his arms and taking a firm grip, he began the trip home.

It was well after dark when they reached the cabin. Sue was completely unconscious, so he carried her into the house. Using some extra blankets, he made a pallet for her on the floor near the fireplace. Cutting up venison into a pot of boiling water, along with a few herbs and seasonings, he hung the pot over the fire. If she could eat some of the meat that would be good but drinking some broth would help rebuild her strength and warm her inside. Last night had been very cold for her to have lain on the ground with very little cover. While the venison cooked, he went outside to tote water to the stall. By the time he came back in, the stew was nearly ready, and Sue was sitting up.

Before supper was finished, he had wet a rag in some warm water and gently cleaned up the wound on her head, getting the dried, caked blood out of her hair. "Mr.

Evers," she said, "how did I get here?"

"I found you at the upper end of the valley," he told her. "What I'd like to know is how you got there, and what happened at your place."

The wound was no more than a crease across the top of her scalp just deep enough to cause some bleeding. A bandage was not even needed, although, she did have a large knot there. She was much more coherent by now and told him the story as best she could remember. "Four days ago, they rode in," she said. "Three of them were Pa's old friends, and the other two fellows I'd never seen before. All was good for a couple of days, and then one evening, they started drinking. Pa had too much and told them about our mine. Before long, they were arguing, and I started to go out with my rifle and tell them they needed to leave, but things quieted down, so I went to sleep."

"Who were these men?" he asked.

"Well, as I told you, I knew three of them. Mike Shelby and Pa had prospected together some years ago when I was small. Rod McCoy and Ed Gray had both worked for Pa on a dig we had year before last. One of the men I didn't know. I heard Ed call him 'Chance,' I think."

"Chance?" repeated Everett. "What did this man look like, Sue?"

"About your age I'd say, very clean-cut, with dark hair," she told him.

"Lord Almighty," he said. "Sue, are you sure your pa is dead? Maybe he was just wounded, as you were."

"No, he's dead," she told him. "I heard a shot, and I guess that's what woke me. Then, as I came outside, I saw him on the ground. I bent down to him, and as he drew his last breath, one of them shot me. I knew I was hit but not bad, so I took out down the valley as I was with no hat, no coat. I had slipped my feet into my boots as I went out with a blanket wrapped around me, thank the Lord. By the time I made it to the end of the valley, I could hear them coming after me, so I just started climbing."

"Are you telling me you came over that ridge with all the snow that's on it?" asked Everett.

"I must have," she said, "to have wound up in your valley."

"I thought you were two valleys over from me," he told her.

"By the trail along the ridge, we are," she said, "but one is a little short valley. It runs north to south, where both of ours runs east to west on either side of a ridge."

He could tell she was tired, so he told her to get some sleep, and he would do the same. "We'll talk more about it tomorrow," he told her. He climbed the ladder to the loft with the weight of the world on his shoulders. How in the world Chance Mason got mixed up with this bunch was something he could not figure out, but it sure sounded like he was. If that was the case, then that meant that he also knew Everett was in this valley. Right now, that didn't bother him much, though. Only a fool would try that rock trail down into his valley, but it was something he would have to watch for. In the next few days, it could warm up enough to make the trail passable.

He woke early, as always, and went down the ladder. There was coffee on by the time he heard Sue stirring in the other room. He walked in and handed her a cup. "Obliged," she said. "Maybe the coffee will clear up my head this morning. I'm sure I done asked you this, Mr. Evers, but how did I get here?"

"It's okay," he told her. "You had quite a rap to your skull."

"Yes, sir," she said, "and I intend to return it."

Everett told her again about seeing her fire at the upper end of the valley, coming there, and finding her. "I still can't believe you came over that ridge," he told her. "There must be ten feet of snow up there."

"In the drifts, there is," she said, "but in most places, it's only about four feet deep."

"That's still something," he said.

"When it comes to saving your bacon, you can and will do a lot of things," she said.

"Sue, I'm real sorry about your pa. I didn't know him well, but he seemed like a standup man to me."

"Pa was a good man," she said, "only he had a way of taking up with the wrong people sometimes. Like that bunch that killed him, and now are sitting on our claim."

"If it's any of my business," he said, "have you found anything there worth dying for?"

"Mr. Evers, it looks better than any claim we ever had. That's probably what got Pa killed, too. When we last went to town, and he had a few drinks, it would be just like him to start talking too much. Then somehow word must have reached Shelby." She stood up and said, "Well, I guess I had best be going."

"Going? Going where?" he asked.

"Well, to get my claim back," she said. "What do you think?"

"Sue, there's five men over there by your account, and we know they have no problem with shooting a woman," Everett replied.

"Only this time, the woman will be shooting back at them," she said.

"You can't go right now," he told her. "I don't know about the trail into your camp, but you would never get a horse up this one. Besides, I found no rifle when I found you."

"No, you wouldn't have," she said. "I left it beside my bed when I came out that night. The wind tried to take my blanket, too, but I knew without it, I would freeze to death. I'm sure you're right about the trails. That is why they are still in our camp because they can't get out," she told him. "One of them had a bottle, and when I saw them start drinking, I knew no good could come from it."

"Sue, if you'll give this weather a few days to clear, I'll loan you a rifle, and the two of us will ride over there and get back what's yours," he said.

"Why would you want to get involved?" she asked. "Is it because I'm a woman?"

"Partly," he said, "but mostly because you're a friend, Sue, and so was your pa."

For five days they waited, and then the temperature began to rise a little, and a weak sun broke through. "If the sun stays out all day," he told her, "It should melt the ice off of the trail enough to get up it. We'll have to go cautious, though," he told her, "Because it may clear your trail, too. That could mean they may be headed our way."

"Maybe," she said, "but if I know them like I think I do, all that's going to be on their minds, for now, is to get at that gold and get away from here as quickly as possible."

"You don't think they will want to find you to make sure there's no witness to what they have done?" he asked.

"Maybe," she said, "only they'll most likely believe I died from my wound, or that I froze to death up on that ridge somewhere."

"Just the same," he said, "we have to be careful."

With a hat and a rifle borrowed from him, Everett thought, *that girl is a sight.* They were in the shed, and while he saddled Mouse, she was putting a blanket on Spook. That's when they heard the lone rider coming very slowly down the trail, and heard his horse slip several times. They didn't show themselves until the rider was in the yard.

Looking out, Sue said, "That's the fellow I told you I didn't know. His name is 'Chase' or 'Chance' or something like that." The man rode up to the bridge, stopped, looked around, then crossed it and rode on to the house.

"Damn," said Everett, looking out there and knowing exactly who that rider was. Quickly, he told Sue that he did know the man and how. He asked if she would stay hidden for a few minutes and cover him. "Give me time to talk to him and see what he says."

"Okay," she said, "but if he makes a wrong move, I'll shoot him out of the saddle."

"Fair enough," Everett told her, "But we go back a long ways, and I'd like to hear him out, at least."

"Howdy, Everett," he said.

"Chance, I thought you were in California," Everett replied.

"Never made it that far," he said. "Everett, can I come inside? I really need to talk to you."

"I think that would be a real good idea, Chance," Everett said. Blocking a shot from the shed with his own body, he told Chance to climb down. "You go on in,"

Everett told him. "I was feeding the stock. I'll finish up and be right in."

Chance went on the porch, and Everett went in the shed door. He told Sue he wanted to hear what Chance had to say, but for her stay by this door and listen. "If you hear him catch himself up in a lie, come on in."

"Then we'll see if he changes his story," she said. He went in through the shed door to the cabin. Chance stood near the fireplace warming his hands.

"You've got you a real good setup here, Everett."

"Worked hard for it, Chance," Everett stated. "You were asked to stay. That would have made lighter work on me, and this would have been half yours, too. So, if you haven't been to California, where have you been?"

"Just around," Chance said, "but I never made it out of Colorado. I stopped in a little town called Grand Junction. Hung around there awhile and met a couple of old boys who told me they had a gold claim up here. They said they just got tired of the solitude and hard work and rode off. If I was willing to help them work it, though, we'd all come back and give it a shot. That was, they said, if nobody had jumped their claim. Anyway, I was getting low on money and figured, hell, why not. If nothing else, I figured it would get me closer back this way, and I could always drop in on you for a meal now and then."

"So, what happened?" Everett asked.

"Well, when we got there, they saw some people on their claim, but they told me they knew who the people were. We would ride in, and they would explain the error these people had made, and they were sure these folks would just move on. We had picked up two other fellows on the way back, and I guess they all knew each other, because they talked among themselves quite a bit. Well, anyway, we set up and after a couple of days they started drinking with this old man that had jumped their claim, and the next thing I knew there was shooting going on, and that old man was killed. Then one of the men I was with shot at the other man. That fellow had stayed away from us the whole time we had been there, so I don't know if he was kin to the old man, just his partner, or what."

"He was neither," said Sue as she stepped inside the cabin. "He is a she, and unless you start telling the whole truth of this, she is fixing to put a hole in you, mister." Sue had that rifle aimed right at Chance, and Everett knew she meant business.

"Chance," Everett said, "this is the other one you spoke of. The old man was her father, Sam Bolen, and this is Sue. I have not known them as long as I've known you. I do know they are good people, and that they've never lied to me like you just did. Now, I think you better start over and give me the whole thing. Either that, or I'm going to step aside and let her do what she wants to."

"Okay," he said, "I reckon I owe you that for the way you were treated back in Leavenworth."

"You don't owe me nothing, Chance, but you do owe this lady the truth about who killed her pa and why."

"Okay," he said. "Like I told you, I met up with these two guys named Mike and Ed, over in Grand Junction one night, and they told me they knew where gold had been found back here. They said it was an old man they had worked with before and his daughter. Mike said all we'd have to do was to throw a scare into them, and the mine would be ours. He told me that the old man had never filed on a claim as long as they'd known him. He would just work one awhile and if it didn't show something, he'd move on. 'This time it's different', he'd said. 'They have been in that same spot for nearly a year, and if there wasn't gold there, they would have done been gone.' I asked them straight out and he said that nobody would get hurt. 'Nay, we just rattle them a little, and they'll move on easy enough,' Mike had said. Anyway, we run into these other two fellows on the way back here. One named Rod McCoy, who had also worked for the old man one time, and a cousin of his named Al Pitts. I kept thinking I knew him from somewhere, but I couldn't place it. We rode on together, and when we came to the trail going into the valley, at first, I thought it was the trail into this valley.

"We rode in and sure enough there was nobody there but two people. The old man was friendly enough with Mike and Ed and told us we could hole up there for a few days as the weather was starting to turn bad. A couple of nights after we got there, one of them broke out a bottle of whiskey and they started drinking. You know me, Everett, I was never much of a drinker, so I just sort of hung back away from the rest. Then, all at once, I heard a shot, and as I came up, I saw the old man lying on the ground near his shelter with a gun in his hand. Then, I guess it was her that came out and went to her pa, and Al shot her, or at least at her."

"He hit me," said Sue, taking off her hat to reveal the wound left by the bullet. "Only he didn't hit me good enough."

Chance continued, "Then she took out running for the hills, and we all chased after her. She got into the mountains, and we lost her. Shelby said, 'To hell with it. Let them freeze up there since that will save a bullet.' Later, I learned that the old man had started talking after he'd had a few drinks and had told Shelby he'd found the mother lode. Told him exactly where the mine was and everything. I guess that's when Shelby decided to kill them both and keep it for himself. He had told the old man that him and the one working with him could leave or die, it didn't matter which one to Al. The old man said to let him get his things and they'd pull out. I guess that's when he got his gun and came back out of the shelter. Al shot him down, and Al is the one that shot her. I swear to you, I never raised a gun against either of them, Everett."

"So, why are you here now, Chance?" Everett asked.

"I got away," Chance answered. "The day after we found the mine, and Shelby saw how rich the ore looked, he started talking about how rich we were all going to be. He went on about, of course, it being his deal, he expected to take a larger share. Al Pitts said, 'Like hell!' Al felt we were all in it together, and besides, he was the one that had killed the old man. Al indicated it would be an even five-way split, or else. They argued about it, and Shelby went for his gun. Al put two slugs into him, before Shelby even cleared leather. That's when it flashed in my mind where I knew him from. I didn't really know him, but I had seen his picture on a wanted poster. Al and some others had robbed a bank in Texas. Later, the other guys were found shot to death in the desert, a couple of them shot in the back. He's a real mean one, Everett, and he don't like to share loot with anybody. I figured that with me not knowing any of them very well, I'd be next. So, I started watching for a chance to get out.

"After a hard day in the mine a couple of days ago, Al started fussing about how he was tired of eating the slop that Ed cooked. I saw it as a chance and told him I'd been a cook back in Kansas for a spell, and I'd be glad to handle it. Well, I cooked yesterday morning, and I guess it impressed him, because yesterday evening he knocked me off early from the mine to go cook supper.

"This morning after breakfast, I told him I was going to clean up some, see what I had to work with for our meals, and then I'd be on to the mine. He bought it, and when they went to the mine, I went straight and saddled my horse and got out of there. If there had still been ice on that trail, I would be dead by now myself. The rest you know."

"What I know," Everett told him, "Is that you were riding with men who shot down an old man and shot this woman to take what was rightfully theirs. Then, when you became concerned for your own life, you came here, which will surely bring trouble to me."

"Maybe you're right," he said, "but I know you can handle Al Pitts. You're probably the only man I've ever seen that was as good with a gun as he is.”

“I intend to take care of him and the rest,” Everett said, “but it’s for her, not for you. I will make you this deal, though, if Sue agrees that she saw no gun in your hand. Otherwise, you can ride out of here right now and take your chances of being caught by them.”

Sue agreed that she had seen no gun in his hand that night.

“Very well, then,” Everett said. “You help us go against them to get her valley and her gold back. If you do that, I will let you ride away from here. It seems like a matter of falling in with the wrong company. It’s that, or I will hold you here until I am through with them and then turn you over to the law in Denver as an accomplice in the robbery and the murder of Sam Bolen.”

“You leave me little choice,” he said.

“I think I leave you a good choice,” Everett said. “Sue, and her pa, are the ones who had no choice.”

“Okay,” Chance said. “What do you want me to do?”

“First, I want to know how well you, and they, are

armed," Everett stated.

"Each one of them has a rifle and a pistol, for sure," he said. "I don't know what guns were in the camp, maybe she can tell you that. As for me, I have a rifle and a pistol, as well."

"Sue, what weapons would be in your camp?" Everett asked.

"Well, Pa had an old pistol," she said, "and a .40-caliber rifle. My .40-caliber is there, too. I had my pistol on when I fled to the mountain, or I would have nothing."

"Very well," Everett said. "We are three people, each with a pistol and a rifle, and are only a little outgunned. The advantage will be if we stay here and hope they come looking for you," he said to Chance. "Do they know about my valley? Have you told them, even in passing, about me being here?"

"I told Shelby that I had a friend here before we started this way, and again mentioned that I thought the trail we were about to go down was to your place," responded Chance.

"Then, it depends on if he told that to Pitts," said

Everett. "If he did, Pitts will know it's close by and will come looking for you. I would prefer it that way, but if they don't show up soon, we'll take it to them."

Sue went part way up the trail to better hear if the men had found it and started down. If they did, she would hide and close in once they reached the camp.

These were vicious men, especially the one called Al Pitts.

Everett would not let them leave this valley alive if they came here. These were the kind of men he despised. They were like Otis Cummins, back in Kansas. They meant to bully and take what they wanted from others instead of working for it themselves. "Chance," he said, "how in God's name could you let yourself get involved with men like them?"

"I don't know, Everett. I just got broke and didn't know anybody there. I guess I got scared, okay?" Chance replied.

"No, Chance, it's not okay. I hoped when you rode away from here, you'd go to California and do big things. Maybe become a sheriff out there or something," said

Everett. "At the very worst, you could have just rode back here. By your own account, you weren't that far away."

"Come back here," Chance said, "with my head hanging down and my tail between my legs like some stray dog?"

"No," Everett told him, "Like a friend needing a hand up. You made the choice to become a stray dog when you hooked up with that bunch."

"Oh, and you always did everything right," he said.

"Me?" Everett said. "Hell, boy, have you lost your mind? I'm the one who stayed in trouble all the time. I'm the one who couldn't even bury my own mother because I was in jail. I had no real job most of the time. You even had a pa to help you grow up right. I didn't."

"You had my pa more than I did," said Chance. "Do you really want to know why he hated you so much, Everett? It was because you were everything his son wasn't. You were a better hunter and tracker. You could shoot and fight. You could stand at the bar and drink half the night like a real man and still whip any one of them in there before you went home. You took no guff from anybody, not even him, and then, not even Otis. I think that's what got him the worst, because even he was afraid of Otis Cummins. Not you, boy. You just beat him down and took what was rightfully yours. Pa hated you for that, but he hated me more for not being like that, like you. Then you went west and made good with the hunting. You know he asked me no less than a dozen times why I couldn't do something like that. He made me his deputy out of pity, Everett. He thought maybe the job would give me the guts to be a real man. When you rode back into Leavenworth, I was glad to see you were alive, but I hated that you'd come back, because I knew he would see what you'd become and be on me even harder."

"Well, I guess the joke was on him in the end, though, wasn't it?" said Everett. "After he was murdered, it was you that brought his killer to justice, Chance. It was you who then quit that job and came all this way to apologize to me. It was you that left here to go on to California. Every one of those things took a man with guts."

"I want to make this right, Everett," Chance said.

"Right with that girl, her pa, and you."

"You owe me nothing," Everett told him, "But you're right in the fact that you owe that girl out there for the killing of her pa. Although you played no hand in it, you played no hand in stopping it either."

"When they come after me, Everett, I'll play that hand," Chance vowed.

"We'll do it together," Everett told him.

By just before dark, the men still had not showed up, so Sue came down the trail to eat and get warm. Whatever was to be would be put on hold.

That night, a north wind brought more than a foot and a half of snow to the valley. In the drift areas, it was as much as eight feet deep. The supplies he'd laid in for winter were meant for one and were starting to show signs of use already. Leaving Sue and Chance at the camp, Everett went out to see if he could scare up any game. He had no luck. Animals are more attuned to nature than people are, so they had probably fed hard for these last couple of days and were now laid up to wait it out. Had he not been preoccupied with other things; he might have noticed their actions. When he got back to the cabin, he was nearly frozen stiff. "It's mean out there," he told them.

"No luck?" asked Sue.

"Not a thing moving," he told her, "Not even the stream. I'll have to take an axe with me to get water for the horses before dark."

"I'll go with you," she said.

She had put a stew together that was almighty good, and from some ground corn meal and a little flour, she had made cornbread to go with it. It was the first cornbread he'd had in some time, and he ate his fill. As Everett stood up from the table, he said, "Thank you, Sue, that was a fine meal." He began to get dressed to go get water for the horses and for Spook.

Sue began to dress warmer, too. "I'll get the dishes," Chance said. When they were out of the house they headed for the stream. Sue told him that she had talked to Chance quite a bit, while Everett had gone hunting.

"Why is he so down on himself?" she asked. "He seems like a nice enough fellow."

"He is," Everett told her. "We've known each other about all our lives."

"He sure has a high opinion of you," she said.

"Chance's biggest problem was his pa," Everett told her. "He was the sheriff back in Leavenworth. He was tough as nails and because Chance wasn't, his pa made life hard on him."

Early the next morning, Everett went out again. This time he went a little farther from the cabin. When he could stand the cold no more, he started for home. About halfway there, a moose came up off the ground almost right under his feet. His first shot was a clear miss, as he had stepped backward very quickly when the moose came up. His next shot hit it in the neck, so he put another one right behind the shoulder to be certain it was dead. As soon as the animal had breathed its last breath, they began to show up in the tree line. Wolves, some of the biggest he had ever seen. They must have been on the trail of the moose themselves when Everett happened on him. "If you boys will wait your turn," he said, "I'll leave something for you." One big old black wolf started edging toward him. He put a shot in the ground near the wolf and shouted at it to go.

The wolf yelped as if he'd been hit. Everett knew he hadn't hit the animal. *Well, this isn't going to be any fun,* he thought. *How can I possibly skin this thing and keep them wolves off me at the same time?* He was just about ready to give the moose to them, when he looked up and saw Sue and Chance coming. "Man, am I glad to see you two," he said as they walked up.

"Dang," said Chance, "that's a lot of meat there, buddy."

"We'll need it," Everett said, "if this weather don't let up soon. I'll skin it out and cut it up if the two of you will keep them wolves off us."

By the time he had the best cuts made into in three packs, the wolves were ready to attack, guns or not. Without wasting any time, they took up their packs and walked away toward home and warmth. They could hear the growling and fighting from the wolves most of the way to the cabin.

The snow slackened a time or two, but the cold held

on and on. On the days of no snow, they all went out hunting in different directions, hoping to scare something up. The moose had been a blessing, but the meat from it was beginning to grow thin already. Sue killed a large buck deer one day, and Chance got another one just a couple of days later. Everett began to see light at the end of the tunnel. He said nothing but wondered how Al Pitts and that bunch fared. Miserably, he hoped. He knew the Bolens had no such shelter as his own and didn't know if they had hunted, smoked, and dried meat and fish as he had.

He had never even thought to ask Sue about their water situation over there. Of course, with this much snow, there would be no problem with water. It was the fish he wondered about. That and the amount of game in their valley. *It would serve them all right if they starved to death over there,* he thought. That, or maybe the weather would take care of them before he had a chance to. When he returned to the cabin, he asked her about their food supply. "It wasn't enough to even do me and Pa all winter," she said.

"Good," Everett replied.

Death In the Valley

Six weeks after Chance had come down the trail, Everett began to feel a warmness in the air. It was still plenty cold, but not as cold. Within another few days, the stream was showing signs of thawing. Although it was still frozen on the surface, the snow had all but melted off it, telling him the water beneath was getting warmer and moving faster.

The sun shining through the window woke him, and he came off the floor like it was on fire. "The trail!" he said to himself and quickly went down the ladder and bolted for the front door. He slung his gun belt on and caught up the buckle. Strapping the gun belt in place, he opened the door. The doorjamb beside his head exploded into a million pieces, sending stinging little splinters into his face and neck. He stumbled backward, slamming the door as he went. Three more shots slammed into the door, although that didn't bother him. He knew he'd built the door a full two inches thick and from seasoned oak. Nothing less than a big bore rifle slug was getting through it. By now, he was sure Chance and Sue were awake and reaching for their rifles.

"Is it them?" Sue asked Everett.

"Well, it sure ain't Santa Claus," he replied. Everett told Sue to cover the front window but to stay low. He sent Chance to cover the window in the kitchen. Racing back up the ladder to his sleeping quarters, he peeked through the shutters. To open them would surely draw fire to himself, so he continued to watch through the slats. Suddenly, he saw a man stand up from hiding and dart to a place ten feet closer to the cabin then drop down again. Everett steadied his aim on the spot where the man had dropped down, and he waited. He heard a crash from a window shattering downstairs and then heard shots from inside and outside exchanged, but he didn't flinch. He waited a minute longer and then saw a head rising from the hiding spot. As he was about to make another dash, Everett stopped him. *He may have lifted that foot in Colorado, but it came down in Hell,* he thought. The man hit the ground, rolled over, didn't and wouldn't move again. Everett went down the ladder and saw that Sue had a bloody bandage tied around her arm. "You hit bad?" he asked her.

"It ain't nothing," she said. "I heard a shot up there,

so I guess we're up against two now."

"That's good guessing," he told her. "Any idea where they are?"

"The shot that got me and the shutter at the same time came from your bridge, I think," she said.

"Somebody was on the bridge?" he asked.

"More like under it," she told him. "I never really saw him."

"Chance!" Everett shouted. "You got any movement out there?" He didn't get an answer and was about to go check on Chance when he heard the rifle speak in the kitchen.

"Not anymore," Chance shouted back. He came in from the kitchen.

"Only one left?" I asked him.

"I got Rod McCoy," he said. "How about you?"

"From the way you described them, I got Ed Gray," Everett said. "That just leaves Al Pitts, then."

"That's the one who killed Pa," said Sue. "You both done got one, so I guess that means he's all mine."

"He's powerful fast, Sue," said Chance. "I think the only man I know that could take him would be Everett."

"Yeah, maybe so," she said, "but I ain't no man." Standing up, she walked to the side of the window. "Pitts!" she shouted. "Your friends are dead. You're all by yourself out there."

They heard Pitts yell first for Ed Gray, and when he got no answer, he shouted for Rod McCoy. "Why don't we end this, just between us," she said, "or are you afraid to face a girl?"

"Is that you, girl? I thought I done killed you one time. Why don't you come out, and we can talk about it?" Pitts said.

"So you can shoot me down before I even see you, like you did my pa, you yellow skunk," Sue replied.

"No," Pitts told her, "you said between us. I'd like to see if you have the guts to back that mouth up, gal. Look here, you tell your boyfriends in there to stay out of it, and I'll face you fair and square."

Looking around at Everett and Chance, she said, "Boys, this one is mine, like I said, but if he should get me, I want you two to cut him to pieces for me and for Pa, okay?"

"Sue, please don't do this," Chance said. "Any man that would accept a callout from a woman would also shoot one."

"I know," she said, "but I intend to be shooting back this time." She walked to the door.

Chance said to Everett, "You can't let her do this."

"I'd hate to try and stop her," Everett said. "Pitts killed her father, tried to kill her, and stole her mine. Besides, I got a feeling about this."

As she walked cautiously out onto the porch, Al Pitts stood up on the far side of the bridge. His pistol was holstered, which surprised Everett. "Girl, you're something else," Pitts said. "Hell, if I wasn't gonna kill you, I might come calling on you. You've got more guts than most men I've known." Sue walked down the steps, and Al slowly crossed the bridge toward her. When they stopped, there was no more than thirty feet between them. Al said, "Look here, girl, I don't really want to kill you. What do you say we kill them two in there? Then,

I'll be a rich man, and you can be my woman. Don't that sound better to you than getting killed?"

"Not really," she told him. "I'd rather be dead than be your woman."

"Girl, there has never been a man born that could beat me," Pitts bragged. At that moment, two hands flashed toward their guns. Two shots sounded like one, echoing through the valley, and Everett was not sure who shot who for a minute. Slowly, Pitts took a step toward Sue, and then he went to his knees.

"Maybe no man could ever beat you," she said, "but I'm no man." Al Pitts fell forward into the snow and died. Sue turned and came back up the steps and in the door.

"I don't believe it," said Chance. "You actually beat him!"

"He wasn't as fast as he thought he was," said Sue. "Most of them ain't. Besides, he attacked before I even had my coffee this morning. Mr. Evers, may we ride over to my valley to make sure my pa got a decent burial?"

"Absolutely, Sue," he said, "on one condition."

"What would that be?" she asked.

"That you call me Everett, and not Mr. Evers, anymore," he said to her.

"Okay, Everett, I think I can do that now," she said.

"That deal still stand for me?" asked Chance. "To let me ride away and call it a mistake on my part?"

"A deal is a deal," Everett told him.

"Well, anyway," Chance said, "for what it's worth, I'm sorry about all of this."

"Go home, Chance," Everett said. "I'm not sure this is where you need to be."

"I think you may be right, Everett. If it's okay with you, I'll ride out as you two go up the trail," said Chance. At the trailhead, he pointed his horse to take him down the mountain and back to Denver. They shook hands, and he told Everett, "If you ever come back toward Kansas, look me up."

Everett told him he would, but both men knew that Everett was at home here, and here is where he would stay. Tipping his hat to Sue, Chance rode away.

"You think he'll really go back home to Kansas?" Sue asked Everett.

"I hope so," he replied. "Chance is a good person deep down and would make them a good sheriff in Leavenworth, but he's not cut from what it takes to live out here."

They found two graves near Sue's shelter when they got to her valley. "I reckon one of them is Pa, and one is that Mike Shelby," she said. They also found several feed sacks full of ore stacked by the side of the shed.

Everett shared with Sue that he figured Al meant to come to Everett's valley and kill them all then ride back here to haul it out using their horses and mules. Sue opened one of the sacks to show him the ore she had told him about and how good it was. "I don't understand," she kept saying. She opened sack after sack then dropped the ore to the ground. "Everett, what me and Pa took into town that day was high grade stuff, if I ever saw any. This ore here don't have enough gold in it to make it worth the effort of getting it out of the ground, much less out of the mountains. "Come on," she said.

Mounting up, they rode to the far end of the valley and as they drew up to a spot, she looked over at Everett. "It looks just like how we left it the last time me and Pa was here," she said. She went to a spot and began to move limbs and brush to expose a piece of tarp covering the mouth of a small tunnel. She bent down, and reaching in, she drew out a chunk of ore. She looked at it for a minute then handed it to him. Everett was no gold miner but you didn't have to be to know this was the real thing. Streaks of gold laced all through the crumbling quartz. "Pa did it," she said. "Even though he was drinking, he smelled them for the skunks they were and told them a tall tale about where the mine was. He must have sent them to the first place we dug back there closer to the shelter. Maybe he figured if they got a look at it, they would just laugh at him and pull out. He never figured on Al Pitts being so greedy."

They covered the tunnel again and started back to her camp. On the way, she told him she couldn't stand to think that her pa was lying in a grave right beside the likes of Mike Shelby. "I'll see to that," Everett told her. While she was busy checking what was left of their shelter and supplies, he removed the stones from one of the graves to find the body of Mike Shelby. Using a piece of tarp, he put the body on it and dragged it about two hundred yards away from camp. Going back to their shed, he found a pick and shovel, and dug what he could into the rocky frozen ground. Rolling Shelby into the shallow hole with his foot, he looked down and said, "You got what you deserved, mister." He shoveled the loose stuff back over Shelby's body and then gathered rocks to cover the grave and keep animals away.

When Everett got back, he told Sue what he'd done. She stated, "So, the one behind the shed is Pa then, I reckon." For the first time, Everett saw tears in her eyes. "I'm sure going to miss him," Sue said. "Everett, I wonder would it be too much trouble if I stayed on at your place until winter is over? I just don't have the heart to stay here without Pa right now."

"You can stay as long as you like," he told her.

She gathered her few belongings and saddled her own horse. He put halters on the other stock, and they rode out of the valley. At the top, she looked back down the trail and said, "I'll be back, Pa, I promise." On the ride back, she said, "Everett, you know that vein Pa found? Well, it probably goes clean through the mountain over to your side."

"I have no doubt of that," he told her. Then he described the nuggets he'd found in the stream soon after he had arrived in the valley. That night, they sat after supper and talked of many things. She told him how she had never known her mother. At least not that she could remember, although her pa had talked about her mother a lot.

"He told Ma how he was planning to come to the mountains and find gold so that they would be better off. Then, she told him I was on the way. He didn't leave her, and the mountains were forgotten about until I was maybe two, and Ma got sick with the fever and died. He could have given me to some family and rode away, you know, but he wasn't that kind of a man. So, he packed me on a mule, and we came to these mountains. Who knows?" she said. "I might have learned to be a grand lady or something if he'd left me behind."

"I happen to think you are one," Everett told her. "To me, a lady isn't how you speak or dress, but how you live your life. Your pa taught you what you really needed, Sue. He taught you how to be a true friend and to stand up for what's right. He showed you how to be strong when you had to and to accept help when it was needed."

She asked what he planned to do about the gold in his valley. "It can't all be reached from the other side," she told him. "From both sides, though, most of it could be gotten."

"I don't want to destroy this valley for it," Everett told her. "I am not a rich man, Sue, but my buffalo hunting did allow me to bank a little money, and with everything this valley gives me, I will probably never have need of more."

They spent the rest of the winter hunting together and sharing in whatever work needed to be done. By the time a person could feel the change in the wind and see it in the grass, they had become very close. One night, after they had finished eating, she said, "Everett, I have to talk to you about something."

"Sure," he told her. "What's on your mind?" She started and stopped a couple of times, and he said, "Sue, just tell me what it is."

"Well, you know I have to go over to my valley," she said. "If I don't work that claim, somebody else will come in and find it."

"I know," he told her, "And I had figured to help you with that."

"How?" she asked. "We both know it's a full time job to take care of your own place."

"If we help each other, it will be possible," he said.

A few days later, they took all of the stock and went to her valley. It was hard work, mining, and it was something he'd never done. Oh, the hard work part he'd done plenty of, but he knew nothing of how to shore up walls or ceilings of a mine shaft, or how to clean the ore so that mostly all you was packing out was gold and not worthless rock. Sue was very knowledgeable about every aspect of mining, and Everett pointed out to her how much she had learned from her father.

Throughout the spring, he stayed at his valley only

enough to keep things up. By near the middle of summer, they were as deep under the mountain as Sue felt safe to go. Their last day in the mine brought little to show for their work, anyway. "It's done here," she said. "Unless you decide later to open a shaft from your side, the rest will stay where it is."

"One day, I might," he told her, "But not now." That night, as he helped her clean and pack the last of her gold, they talked of their plans for the next day and about getting her gold into town. "It will take every horse and mule we have," he said, "to haul it to Denver, and I will ride there with you, Sue. As soon as you are through at the assayer's office, I must take Spook and leave. I will need to come back to my valley as quickly as possible. If word gets out as to what you brought in, there will be people crawling all over these hills within a matter of hours, and I'll not have them in my valley."

"Everett, I was intending to give you half of whatever the gold brings," she said.

"I am not in need of it," he told her. "My valley provides me with almost all the things I need. Will you be coming back to your valley?"

"I will come back," she said, "to see Pa again, but I'll have no reason to stay there anymore. Pa and me, we never planned to stay and live there like you have, and with the gold and Pa gone, why stay?"

True to his word, after all her gold was unloaded, he made ready to leave. They sat in front of the assayer's office a minute, and he said to her, "When you come to see your pa, don't forget to look in on a friend."

"I would never forget to do that," she replied, and he rode away back to his valley.

*

Fall came early, and he was glad. That meant bad weather up high, and that would help to stem the flow of prospectors. In the two weeks following Sue cashing in her gold, he had run ten men from his valley at gunpoint and buried one who would have it no other way. Still, he managed to get a good supply of meat cured for winter, and plenty of firewood moved closer to the cabin. As accustomed to being alone as he'd gotten out there on the plains, he soon found that he so had grown used to the company of both Sue and Chance. During the days, not so much, but at supper it was very lonesome, at times. He knew that after a while, he would go back to the way he had been before they came. Sue had not yet been back to her valley, at least that he knew of, and he felt sure she would have come to see him if she had returned. At times, he would catch a movement from the corner of his eye and turn that way, expecting to see her standing there. *What in the world is wrong with you, Everett Evers?* he thought. *It's not like you were in love with the girl or something.* That same sentence played over and over in his head all that night. By the morning light, while he was having his coffee, it slid through his mind again.

He set the cup on the table and said out loud, "Well, do you?" The answer he got was, he just wasn't sure. Was he in love with her or was it just a matter of missing her company? He sat at the table and put on his boots. He was going to Denver to find her and find out. If he saw her right now, he would know for sure if what he felt was love, or if he was just missing a friend. It was the craziest thought he'd ever had in his life, but still, he knew he was going to do it. Stamping into his boots, he pulled open the door to go to the stalls and was met by a white world all around him. Winter had come to the valley yet again. *That's okay,* he thought. *If it does like it did last year, it will be gone in a few days, and I will go then.*

The weather in the mountains of Colorado is everchanging. There was no few days of warmup this year, just day after day of cold, and most of them held some snowfall. For the first two weeks, he was still able to hunt a little, but then it became so cold and so deep with snow that he found himself limited to just the cabin and the shelter of Mouse and Spook. *So, this is a real winter up here in these mountains,* he thought. The first one was just to break him in for mountain life. Then, last winter, as bad as the weather was, at least he had the help and company of both Sue and Chance. He slept often and ate a little each time he woke up. By the end of the first month, his supply of coffee was nearly gone, and he had started to ration himself.

He would make a fresh pot early when he got up, and then add a little to the old grounds for a pot in the evening. He also put this plan in action for his food stores, although there was probably no need for it. Right about then, he was thankful for having never picked up the smoking habit or caring much for alcohol. By now, he would surely have been out of both and having to deal with a wanting for it.

For over two months, every time it seemed like it was about to be finished, he would wake up to another snowfall. By the time warm weather finally came again to the valley, he had thought plenty about Sue. Enough to realize that he was simply lonely for the company. He was not in love with her, and obviously she had none of those feelings for him, or she would have come back from Denver, as she'd said she would. *Why would she, though?* he wondered. She was now a wealthy woman and could go anywhere and live as she wished, and apparently that was what she was doing.

With the warmer weather came the cleaning up of the mess that winter had left behind. Limbs broken from the trees by ice and snow were dragged to his supply of firewood. Riding one day to the far end of the valley, Everett could see a change in the ridge between his valley and the one where the mine had been. Winter, in its freezing and thawing of the ridge, had caused the tunnel cut in the other side to collapse. Surface boulders as big as his cabin had rolled down to the valley floor.

High up the bare slope, he could see a large crack in the mountain itself. While watering Mouse before heading back, he could see the stream bottom. It was littered with fresh gold nuggets and pieces of gold-bearing ore. He supposed the caving in of the mine had pushed them there. For a brief moment, he considered mining it now, and going away like Sue had done. It was a thought he would never act on, of course. Maybe she and her father had been in their valley only for the gold they had found there, but he was truly happy here. He had no gold when he found this place, and he needed no gold now to keep him there.

Two weeks into spring, he made that ride to Denver, taking Spook along as he would be buying supplies. At the store, John Pate asked if he'd had a rough winter. "Well, it wasn't a pleasant one," Everett told him, "But I survived it."

"Have any trouble with miners after that Bolen girl

made her strike?" Pate asked.

"Had to put a couple off," Everett said. "One wouldn't be put off, so I put him down."

"That friend of yours came through town back in the summer and went to see the sheriff about what had happened with old Sam getting killed. I thought he'd gone to California," said Pate.

"No, he never made it that far," said Everett, "and it's a good thing, too. If he'd not been there to help with them boys that killed Sam, they may have got his daughter, and me, too."

"He told me he was headed back to Kansas," Pate said. "That was a bad deal about old Sam."

Everett said, "The greed of man knows no bounds, until someone points them out."

"According to your friend, you're pretty good at showing them the error of their ways," said Pate.

"What of Miss Bolen?" Everett asked. "Is she still in town? She did not return to the mountains, and I was concerned."

"She sold her gold, and shortly after that, she left town on the stage," said Pate.

"On the stage?" Everett repeated. "Are you sure? She didn't strike me as the stage rider type. She handled a horse as well as any man I've ever met."

"Just the same," Pate said, "she left Denver on the stage. Some folks, when they come into money, completely change."

"Well, good luck to her," Everett told John Pate. He loaded the mule and started for home. He knew when he left town, he'd never get home before dark, but he had no desire to stay in town.

Most of that summer, he explored the mountain trails around him. When he had first come into the mountains and found his valley, he went no farther to see what else there was to be seen. In all his searching, though, he found no other valley to compare with the one he had. As the leaves began to change, and color came again to the trees of the valley, Everett started once again to prepare for winter. It was a cycle, but then so was life down in town, and here at least other than the weather, he had some control over his life.

In the first week of August, he rode once again to Denver. He bought what the valley could not provide, but that he enjoyed. Mainly that was his coffee and flour, because he did like his biscuits at breakfast and supper. John Pate filled his order, which would be tied behind his saddle, as it was only a small bundle. "I heard your friend came back to town yesterday," Pate told Everett.

"Chance is back here?" Everett asked.

"No," answered Pate, "your other friend, Miss Bolen."

"Good," he said. "It's good to know she is safe."

"Don't know how long she'll stay safe," John said.

"What does that mean?" Everett asked. "Have you heard about somebody that means to do her harm?"

"I don't know about harm," Pate said, "but then I guess you haven't seen her yet," he said, chuckling.

"No, I haven't seen her," Everett said, "and don't expect I will unless she comes to visit me at my home.

That's where I am heading, and with luck I will not be back before spring."

"You really should take time to see her," said Pate. "You may be as surprised as the rest of us were."

"When last we spoke, she said she would come to see me and visit the grave of her father," Everett told him. "I guess if and when she gets ready, she will." He picked up the bundle and went to his horse. "That man has a mental problem," he told Mouse.

While he was cooking supper, he heard a lone horse on the trail down. *Now who would that be?* he wondered. *It is late in the evening and the year for visitors, even if there was anyone to visit me.* He heard the *clop*, *clop* as the horse came over the bridge, and setting his supper to the side, he picked up his rifle and went to the door.

He went out the door, and there sat a lady riding sidesaddle. Well, he had seen this done back in Kansas, but to see it up here in the mountains on these narrow trails was a sight to behold. "Howdy, ma'am," he said, "I believe you may have taken a wrong turn, a very wrong turn. If you were looking for Denver, you missed it by near forty miles."

"I've taken no wrong turn, sir. Now, would you be so kind as to help a lady down?" Something about the voice made him think of Sue. It sounded like her, but without the brassy, tough edge that she had. He went to the side of her horse, and only then did he see it was Sue, only it wasn't. Well, at least not the way he'd always known her to be. The woman on the horse wore a fancy dress and makeup and had her hair all fixed in place with pins. She had said nothing about who she was, so he decided to play along with whatever it was Sue was up to.

"Are you that new mail-order bride I sent away for?" he asked as they started up the steps.

"I ain't no durn mail order bride, Everett. It's me, Sue," she said. "If I thought you really had sent for one, I'd nail your hide to the smokehouse wall, Everett Evers!"

"What are you doing here?" he asked.

"Well, I'd be glad to tell you if you'd invite me in for some coffee, or have you no manners at all?" Sue said.

"Of course," he said. "Madam, would you be so kind

as to join me for a cup of coffee?"

"You beat everything, you know it," she said as she went past him and poured herself a cup of coffee. Once at the table, she took off what he supposed some women called a hat, although he couldn't imagine why they would.

"How are you?" he asked, when he sat down across from her.

"Plumb irritated," she said. "I went all the way to New York and paid good money to learn how to be a proper lady, then I ain't back around you for ten minutes, and you done went and undid it all."

"Why would you do something like that, anyway?" he asked.

"Well, you never in all our time together, treated me like more than a kid sister, and I thought maybe it was because of how I was. So, after I sold my gold, I decided it was worth a try to learn how to dress and talk like a real lady. I thought maybe then you'd notice me."

"I noticed you from the first time we ever met," he told her.

"Why didn't you ever act like it?" she asked him.

"I don't know," he said. "Maybe I wasn't sure how I felt about you."

"Well, just how do you feel about me, Everett?" she asked.

"Well, I love you," he told her. "What I don't know, is do I have a right to? After you went away, I missed you something awful, and one time I was fixing to come to Denver looking for you, but I got snowed in. Besides, you never let on that you felt more than friendship for me."

"Everett, I've known I was falling in love with you since that first night I spent in your camp," said Sue. "You treated me like a real lady, and the Lord knows, I ain't one. With you treating me that way, I thought that's the kind of woman you wanted for a wife."

"What would I do with a woman like that?" he said. "I intend to live in this valley the rest of my days. Do you think a city woman would want that? Both of us having to work all summer to get ready for winter, then to set here snowed in half of it. I don't. Now, you have all that money from your gold and could go anywhere you want to. I thought you might want to see all the things you missed roaming these hills with your pa. You wouldn't have to worry about firewood and hunting in order to eat."

"That's not what I want," she told Everett, "And if the money is the problem, I'll give it away. Finding gold was Pa's dream, not mine. My dream was to find a man that would love me and respect me as an equal. Most men can't seem to do that. They want a wife who can't shoot as well as them or tote a log to the fire big enough to last all night. I was beginning to give up on that, until you came into your valley that day. You treated me like a lady, asking me to take your shelter for the night. When I said 'no,' you didn't make out that you could stand the cold, but I couldn't because I was a woman. Then, when Chance was here, you left him at the cabin and went hunting with me. Mostly, though, it was the day I was going out to face Al Pitts. I could read fear for me on your face, but you knew I had to do it myself, and you let me. I love you, Everett, and I'd be proud to be your wife if that's what you want. If it's not, I'll ride out in the morning and not bother you again."

At breakfast, neither one of them had much to say. After he'd finished eating, Everett started to the door.

"Where are you going?" asked Sue.

"To saddle your horse," he told her, and then he went out. She had changed out of that awful dress into clothes she was more comfortable in. She packed what few things she had brought along and went out the front door. There stood Everett with her horse, but his was also saddled.

"Are you going somewhere this morning?" she asked.

"I'm riding to town with you," he said. "I couldn't expect a fine lady like yourself to live up here with me without being properly married, could I?"

"Do you mean it, Everett, do you really want to marry me?"

"As much as I love this valley," he answered, "I wouldn't want to stay here without you. I need to ask you, though, are you through riding sidesaddle?"

"You don't have to worry about that," she told him. "I thought I would kill myself before I got here yesterday."

The preacher in Denver was more than happy to marry them, and after a trip by the store to get a few things, and to tell John Pate about their marriage, they headed back to their valley. They hunted and fished together for many years in that valley, along with raising three sons. The two oldest boys, named Sam and Jack, went to the city when they were just in their teens to find employment and to make a life for themselves. The mountain life was just not how they wished to live.

The youngest son, Coy, stayed there with them until they both passed away. Sue went first, after a fall from her horse, when she was almost sixty years old. Everett died in his sleep at the age of sixty-eight. Shortly after his father died, while Coy was doing some cleaning in the house, he found a letter addressed to him. It was in his pa's handwriting, and it told him about a bank account in town that was to be split three ways with his brothers. *"This money,"* the letter read, *"is from a gold mine your mother and grandfather had in the next valley over."* The letter went on to say that ownership of the valley they lived in belonged solely to Coy, as he seemed to love it as much as they had. Then, as he read on, his father told him about the gold mine from the other valley years ago. The letter also told him that if he wanted to find it, there was gold at the head of this valley, too. *"I never wanted to destroy the valley,"* it read, *"but if you are reading this that means the valley is yours, and you may do as you wish. Your mother and I were very proud of all of you boys, and I'll miss being with you, but I miss being with her, too.* The letter was signed, *"Pa."*

Coy rode to town to let his brothers know of their father's letter. Together they went to the bank, but instead of splitting the money three ways, Coy took only a small part and split the rest between his brothers. He told them it was all he would ever want, as the valley supplied almost everything a man would ever need.

The End